Return to
Wonderland

LOOKING GLASS SAGA

BOOK ONE

Return to Wonderland

TANYA LISLE

SCRAP PAPER ENTERTAINMENT

ISBN-13: 978-1-988911-67-0

Scrap Paper Entertainment
www.scrappaperentertainment.com

Contents

CHAPTER 1

Lucena Academy

AT LAST, ALICE had made it.

For years she dreamed of attending Lucena Academy, the prestigious boarding school that her older sister, Lori, went to. It sounded like the best place in the world, complete with grounds to run through, a garden that she didn't have to pull weeds out of, and a forest that, though it was off limits, was at the center of many tales that Lori brought back with her on breaks.

There was also school, of course. That was what her mother and father were more concerned with. The school had the best teachers, the best facilities, the best resources, and the best families attending so that they could succeed.

All of those things were wonderful, but Alice looked forward to the people the most. She could already see old friends meeting up around her as they were dropped off by their parents, wandering back to their dorms or just standing around and chatting. She didn't know what to say to any of them or how to approach them, but she was going to meet so many people here. She could hardly wait.

"Alice," her mother said, bringing her attention back to the car. Her mother and father were there to see her off, though both looked worried.

Alice went back to them, trying to keep her smile more contained. They were worried, she knew, and she was going to do her best to make sure that they had nothing to worry about. She gave her mother an awkward hug, pulling back a moment later with a smile. "Thank you," she said. "I'll be on my best behaviour, I promise."

That was enough for her mother, who smiled back. "Have a good semester," she said, kissing Alice on the top of her head and smoothing out her blond hair behind the black headband she used to keep most of it out of her face. "And study hard. We don't want to get any phone calls from the school about you."

Her father was less content. He didn't think Alice was ready yet, she knew. He thought she should still be home-schooled for a little while longer, kept away from people who might think she was odd. But she'd done so well at being normal that she was certain he would have nothing to worry about.

"No one will call about me," she said. "I promise."

"They better not."

She smiled back at him and hugged him as well. He pulled away first, nodding down at her, then turning to her mother. "We're going to be late if we stay much longer. You'll find your way?"

"Yes," she said, letting her smile widen. She loved her parents, but she was anxious for them to leave. When they left, she'd be able to go out and explore. With the entire campus so close behind her, she could hardly wait.

"Have a good semester," her father told her, getting back into the car. "We'll see you at Christmas."

"We love you, dear," her mother added as she followed him in.

"I love you, too," Alice told her just as the door closed. She stood on the curb with her suitcase and waved as her parents drove away. She waited until they were out of sight before turning back to the school.

Lucena Academy. At last.

She resisted the urge to run through the garden, instead walking through the gate and down the path with her single suitcase in tow, taking in the flowers and shrubbery on either side. The air filled with the sounds of people, so many people that were wandering all around her. She wanted to talk to them all, but didn't know what to say. Hello might be fine, but they looked busy, probably on their way to find their dorms or catching up with old friends.

Instead, she pinched the inside of her wrist, just to be sure that this was all real.

"Pardon me."

It was going to be great actually having friends. She never had any back home, except maybe her tutor. At least, Ms. Miller had always been kind to her. Lori taught her not to mistake kindness for friendship, so she was never quite sure if she could count the woman among her friends. Ms. Miller was quite a bit older than Alice as well, so Alice doubted that she enjoyed their time together as much as Alice did.

"Excuse me, miss."

She spotted the church on campus on the far side of the garden. Perhaps she should start going on Sundays. At home, Alice had always been too busy seeing her doctors on Sunday to attend church with her family. Not that she really knew that it was a good idea. She didn't really know much about what she was supposed to do there. It was far too many years ago that she'd actually been to one.

Before the doctors.

She felt a hand on her shoulder and stopped walking. "Excuse me," he said again.

Alice turned and had to look up. The other person was a boy much older than she was, wearing the seniors' uniform.

His black hair was cut short and he smiled, looking her carefully over with his brown eyes.

"Hello," Alice said with a smile, not completely certain what she was supposed to do in this situation. "My name is Alice. And you are?"

He smiled. "Evan," he told her. "I saw your parents drop you off. You're a first year, aren't you? Grade seven?"

"Yes, I am."

"Your parents didn't want to see you in?"

"They're busy," Alice told him. "They needed to get back to work."

While Alice's smile did not falter, Evan's did for a moment. He recovered quickly, though Alice wasn't sure why he looked so disappointed in that moment.

"Let me help you in," he said, gently taking the handle of her suitcase and leading the way to the dorms. "Have you taken the tour already?"

"No," she said. "But my sister told me a lot about the school already. I can't wait to go looking around."

"Your sister?"

"Lori," Alice told him, a little sad. "She's not back this year. My parents let her go to Europe without telling me. But that's all right. It didn't concern me, so I shouldn't worry about it. And I'm sure she'll call once she thinks I'm more settled in."

"I'm sure she will," Evan said.

Alice let out a breath and tried to focus again on the happier things. She had finally been allowed to leave the house. She was going to an actual school and she was going to have a roommate and maybe that roommate would become her friend. She might actually manage to get more than one friend while she was here. She could go to a real school and actually be with other people her own age and maybe even never see another doctor again.

"These are the dormitories for middle school," Evan told her as they reached the large, U-shaped building. There were a lot of other kids here and Alice noticed that a lot of them were with their parents or older siblings. She was suddenly grateful that Evan was there, so she wasn't the only one there without someone older helping her.

"Let's get you checked in." He led her to a table in the back of the large foyer. She was almost certain when there weren't people around that this would actually be used for something, but right now there were other kids everywhere with their parents and without, some of them sobbing and some of them looking deliriously happy and some looking almost bored.

"Name?" the girl behind the desk asked. She was about Evan's age, brown hair with glasses. She looked up and looked from Alice to Evan, her eyes settling on him. "Hey Evan. She doesn't look related."

"Just giving her a hand."

"You know the rules."

"Of course," he said, Alice catching a hint of deviousness in his grin.

"My name is Alice Liddell," Alice said.

The girl looked down the list and found her name on it, fetching her key from a box beside her. "Here you go. It looks like your roommate's already checked in. An Adrianna..."

She paused, looking back at Evan with irritation. Evan did his best to ensure his face did not change, but Alice could tell from the satisfied look in his eyes that everything was going according to plan, whatever that plan was.

"I'll show you up," Evan said, picking up Alice's suitcase and leading her to the stairs.

She followed behind him as he quickly skirted around the corner and down the hall, avoiding a knot of girls Alice's age talking to an older girl also in the senior's uniform. She tried to keep up as Evan led the way down to the hall, past several doors that had been left open and girls inside either alone or nervously getting to know one another.

"Do you think my roommate will be nice?" Alice asked, slowing down as she realized what was about to happen.

Introducing herself to a senior was one thing. She'd probably never see him again. She didn't think he'd even still be here helping her. But her roommate, she would be sharing a room with her for a whole year, possibly all through middle school. Alice needed to make sure that whoever she ended up with didn't hate her.

"I'm sure she's a very nice girl," Evan said, stopping just before the door before the end of the hall. He gestured to allow Alice to go ahead of him into the room.

Alice took a deep breath and walked in, knowing she was probably as ready as she was going to be. She scanned the dorm, finding two beds, two desks and two dressers propped up against opposite walls and a window on the far side next to a washroom that had been left wide open.

On one side, a girl with long black hair had her back turned as she went through her open suitcase and was getting her clothes out. She didn't even seem to notice that anyone else was there, humming to herself.

Though she was too nervous to say anything, Evan was not. "Addie!" he said, following behind Alice. "What a surprise. Are you in this room?"

The other girl stood up a little straighter at the sound of his voice and turned around, pulling the ear buds from her headphones out and smiling back at Evan, then down at Alice.

"This is Alice," Evan said to her, stepping around Alice

to stand between the two of them. "Alice, this is my sister, Adrianna. It looks like the two of you are going to be roommates this year."

Alice, though she was almost certain Evan had planned this, was willing to overlook the setup. "Hello," she said, offering a hand to Adrianna.

Adrianna took it and shook. "Hi," she said.

"It's nice to meet you."

Alice heard a soft thump behind her and turned to see what it was. Evan was sitting on the other bed next to her suitcase. "Don't mind me," he said, looking around the room. "You two should talk. Get to know each other. Settle in."

"Thank you for helping me in," Alice said. It felt awkward having Adrianna's older brother watching over them, like when she had to prove to her father and the doctors that she wouldn't slip up again. She had gotten quite good at passing those tests, but she wasn't sure what she had to do to pass this one yet.

"No problem," he said. "My pleasure, really. I just—"

"Ahem."

They all turned to the door where a woman in her mid twenties stood, leaning against the doorframe and glaring at Evan. She was dressed in jeans and a long shirt, her curly red hair tied back with a few strands falling over her green rimmed glasses.

"Hello Miss Amanda," Evan said, smiling brightly and getting to his feet.

"Mister Case," she said, not ready to take any of his attempts at charm. "I believe you know the rule about boys in the girls' dorms."

"I do," he said, smiling and meeting her eyes. "Door open at all times and only to visit family, correct? And, seeing as this here is my younger sister and the door is open, I don't believe I'm breaking any rules."

Miss Amanda looked from Evan to Alice sceptically, then over to Adrianna. She looked down to a clipboard that she had in her hands and nodded, a wry smile turning into a genuine one as she lowered the clipboard back down. "Alice and Adrianna, I take it?" she asked.

The girls nodded.

Miss Amanda smiled at both of them. "My name is Miss Amanda. I'm one of the advisors for your floor and one of five advisors for the girl's dorms. We'll have a chance to sit and talk over the next week, but for now, know that you can come to me if you need anything, okay?"

Adrianna smiled and said, "Okay." Alice just nodded.

"I'll leave the two of you to unpack. In half an hour we're all meeting downstairs and are going to head to the assembly."

"Thank you, Miss Amanda," Alice said.

Miss Amanda smiled back. "You're very welcome," she

said before she went to the door and leaned against the frame, her gaze on Evan.

"I think I should let the two of you get to know each other," Evan said, getting up from the bed and joining Miss Amanda at the door. "I'll check on you again later."

"Thanks," Adrianna said as Evan and Miss Amanda left.

Alice and Adrianna went to their respective sides of the rooms, Alice opening up her suitcase and laying her clothes out on her bed. Adrianna fidgeted with a few of the things she brought, putting them away into her dresser or closet.

"Your brother seems nice," Alice offered. "He saw me when my parents dropped me off and showed me in."

"Evan's really nice," Adrianna said. "He's usually really busy with stuff, though, so I usually ask Joe first if I need something."

"Joe?"

"My other brother. Well, one of my other brothers."

"How many brothers do you have?" Alice asked, taking a seat on her clothes to look at Adrianna while they talked.

Adrianna sat down and thought about it. "There's seven of them, but only six are here. Ryan graduated. Then there's Evan. Then Joe and Travis. Then Mike, Mark, and Matt."

"You have three brothers with names that all start with M?"

Adrianna shrugged. "They don't really. They all just

decided to go by their middle names because they thought it was funny and haven't stopped yet. Joe and Travis keep saying they will one day, but they don't think so. What about you? Do you have any brothers?"

Alice shook her head. "Just a sister. Lori's not coming this semester, though. My parents are letting her go to school in London for a while."

"That's so cool!"

Alice smiled and looked away. "Yeah."

"I wonder if any of my brothers know her. We should ask when you meet them."

"Meet them?" Alice asked, feeling her heart drop.

Adrianna nodded. "Don't worry, they're all really nice. Except sometimes Mike, Mark, and Matt. But usually they're really nice."

Alice didn't feel any better and went back to unpacking. Adrianna kept talking about her brothers. Mike, Mark, and Matt were in trouble a lot for pulling pranks. Travis was on a few of the sports teams and his twin, Joe, was in a band during the summer as a singer. Evan was on the student council and wanted to get into politics.

Though Alice nodded and tried to ask questions and seem like she was paying attention, she could feel her stomach tying up in knots. She wanted Adrianna to like her, but now there was so much more to worry about. What if one of her brothers didn't like her? Would they tell Adrianna not to be friends with her? She didn't know what she was even supposed to do when she met a potential friend's brother.

She wished Lori was here. Lori would know what to do. Unfortunately, she didn't even know how to get in touch with her big sister.

Adrianna was about to start talking about Ryan when they both realized the time. They went downstairs to meet the other new girls, most of whom looked a little nervous and uncertain about what was going on as they followed the five advisors for the dorms to the theatre.

The assembly itself was nothing that interesting. Alice and Adrianna chatted quietly, Alice asking Adrianna about what she liked to do. Really, she hoped Adrianna wouldn't keep talking about the other people that Alice was certain she was going to have to impress before the end of the year.

On stage, they recounted the proud academic excellence of the school and assured the new students that they would prosper here. There wasn't much more to it, much of the rest reminding everyone of the ground rules of the school and a brief introduction to how the system worked.

As a boarding school, there were the students who would be there all the time and day students who went home after classes. Those who lived on campus had dorm advisors who would take care of their needs, including any personal issues they may have to deal with. The advisors were fully equipped to deal with anything they might want and they would organize outings so they wouldn't get too restless on campus.

Alice and Adrianna were only barely paying attention until the student council took the stage. She saw Evan on stage as treasurer of the student council and the council was getting ready for several events that would happen this year. They all seemed quite enthusiastic about it all and, though Alice almost expected it, he made no mention or warning to anyone to not trouble his little sister. Instead, he kept looking over at another section of the auditorium where three brown haired boys were sitting.

They were dismissed soon afterwards. Though Alice and Adrianna got up and left together, the crowds of students scrambled around them, moving in waves and Alice found herself following a crowd that left her in a hallway she didn't recognize. She lingered at the side of the hall as the rest of the students dispersed, all of them looking like they knew where they were going, but Alice didn't recognize any of them.

She took a deep breath and kept calm. She could just retrace her steps. She turned back and tried to figure out where she had come from, finding a set of stairs. She didn't remember passing a set of stairs on the way here, but she wondered what was up there. There was a deep blue carpet leading up to a higher floor. It looked like it had windows.

Curiosity won out over worries about being lost and she went upstairs to see a hallway that led to a locked door. The windows that lined the wall showed the rooftop where it looked like someone had started a garden years ago and abandoned it.

"Finding yourself lost again in a strange new world?" a voice said, sounding strangely familiar, something from a long time ago. "But then, what is lost? If you find your way in the end, were you ever lost in the first place, or merely taking a detour?"

She looked around for where the voice was coming from. What she eventually found was a face that slunk around the corner, followed by the rest of their body. It was a boy a few years older than she was, possibly several years, with purple hair that seemed to go everywhere, wild and equally purple eyes and a mouth that was a little too wide for his face grinning from ear to ear. It was the mouth with the voice that made her remember where she'd heard it before.

Alice pinched the inside of her wrist, but he didn't go away.

"I remember you," Alice said, feet backing away a step. "You were a cat the last time I saw you."

"Was I?" he asked, puzzling over it. He looked down at himself. "I do appear not to be a cat right now. Appearances are meant to be deceiving, though. I still feel very much like

I am a cat and merely borrowing the form of a school boy for now. Or perhaps it's the boy borrowing my mind."

"You still speak in riddles."

"If I did not, would I still be myself? I am quite pleased with being myself, you see, and would rather prefer not to be someone else. Other people are terribly dreary." He thought for a moment, then smiled wide at Alice. "Though I admit," he said, slinking around behind her, "I do prefer being a cat."

When he appeared on her other side, he was what she remembered him as. The large cat from Wonderland, covered in swirling purple stripes, smiled back at her, showing all of his teeth.

Alice flinched at the sight of him, the ghost of a pain running through her arm. The Cheshire Cat had found her again and was sitting here before her. She promised that she would not talk about Wonderland and would not try to say Wonderland was real, but what was she supposed to do when Wonderland found her?

"I need to go," Alice said, her heart pounding in her ears. She turned and went back to the stairs as quickly as she could without running.

"I see," he said, slinking back around her feet to stop her from going further, his tail snaking along her leg. "Little Alice is lost and would like to find her way back, but you're an awfully long way from home. Sent away for speaking too much of a place which may not even exist. Tsk tsk."

Alice tried to step away from him and remove her feet, but he continued to purr and wind himself up around her body.

"I wonder if they made you forget. You remember me, but do you remember the rest? And if you've forgotten, did any of it really happen? Was it real? I wonder. What have they done to you since you left us? To you, did Wonderland ever exist?"

"It does exist, you stupid cat!" she snapped at him. Her hands went back to her mouth immediately, her eyes darting around to make sure no one heard her.

"Oh, so you do remember," he said with a bit of a sad drawl. "But the Wonderland of now is not the Wonderland of fun and games it used to be. All things change in time, young Alice, but Wonderland has not changed for the better. It is no longer a pleasant place and I did well to take my leave when I did. Though I am considering returning."

"That's good," Alice said, trying to untangle herself from the cat, who was now winding himself up under her arms. She needed to get away from Wonderland. She wasn't supposed to even be thinking about Wonderland anymore. "You belong there."

"Belong," the cat laughed. "Perhaps. Perhaps it is where many maddening things belong. You are mad too, young

Alice, and don't you forget that. Perhaps you belong in Wonderland with me."

The Cheshire Cat slunk off of her and onto the railing, watching her as she backed away from him and started to head down the stairs. "If you wish to return," he said, "if only for a moment, there is a way. It will be my half birthday present to you, if you wish to accept such a gift."

Alice stopped on the stairs, her breath catching in her throat. "I don't think I'll be going back again," Alice said, not looking back at him. "I think I endured enough from my last visit to last an entire lifetime."

"If you wish, young Alice," he said, his voice silky as it seemed to slip past her ear. "But your gift has not yet arrived. There is a month yet until you can even decide whether or not you will accept."

She turned back but the cat had vanished.

CHAPTER 2

A Chat With The Cat

ALICE WAS SURPRISED how easy it was to get used to the routine. At home, her tutor taught her all day and they covered topics as they pleased. Here, there were times when they did each subject and those subjects didn't bleed into one another like they used to. When questions were posed to the teacher, they had to raise their hands and the teachers had the option to ask them not to ask yet.

For the most part, Alice watched in classes rather than participated. She wrote down what she was supposed to, but she was still confused about the etiquette for class in the social sense. There was a hierarchy building already and she was having trouble wrapping her head around how or why it was happening. She was just happy to sit next to Adrianna in her classes, who willingly partnered with her for any assignment.

While none of the classes were particularly difficult yet,

the only class she really enjoyed so far was English. Even trying to figure out why some people were more popular than others seemed to fade away in that class, her attention instead on the poetry they started out the semester with. She liked trying to find the stories in them.

At the end of the first week their teacher, Ms. Bilamora, passed out notebooks near the end of class. "As I'm sure you're all aware, the only way you get good at something is with practice," she said. "The only way you're going to get good with English is if you practice writing it every day. Starting today, I want each of you to write one page in this journal until the end of the semester. You can write whatever you want. A journal, a story, your dreams, poetry, anything. You just need to get in the habit of writing regularly. At the end of the semester, I'll check for blank pages and mark based on that."

The class let out a groan. Alice wrote her name on the cover where it asked for it and put it in her bag. The bell rang moments later and she left with the rest of the class, Adrianna at her side.

"Do you know what you're going to write?" Adrianna asked.

Alice shrugged. "I don't know yet. You?"

"Dreams seem like an easy thing to write about," Adrianna said. "You think she's going to read them?"

"I don't know," Alice said. "My tutor always read all of my work before."

"You should write about your dreams too!"

Alice hesitated. "I don't really have dreams all the time," Alice said. It was true that since she'd gone to see some of the doctors, she'd stopped having regular dreams. Some of the medicines they'd put her on and some of the therapies left her dreamless for a while.

"You can write about them when they happen."

Alice nodded but said nothing else, walking with the group of students back to their dorms. Her dreams would not be good to write about. When her dreams came now, they were filled with images of drowning in tears and playing cards threatening to cut off her head. She hadn't dreamt about Wonderland in years, but the Cat had brought it back. Still, she was determined not to think about it.

After school, they had a habit of going back to their dorms and taking over their common area to work on their homework before dinner. The older years in the dorms did not do their work until after dinner, off socializing at this time, so they had free reign of the common area.

Alice took her usual seat at a large table and everyone else took theirs. Adrianna sat to her left and they were soon joined by the rest. Sarah, a short blonde girl who seemed to always have something to complain about despite how often she smiled, sat on Alice's other side. Robert, who seemed to spend most of their homework sessions staring at Adrianna, sat across from them with his roommate, Kevin. Sarah's roommate, Heather, joined them late, taking the last empty seat as they spread their books out.

"Can you believe it?" Sarah asked. She had Ms. Bilamora as well, but at a different time. "A page a day! And not even on the computer. By hand!"

"I know," Robert agreed with a groan. "Do you know what you're going to do for it, Adrianna?"

"I think I'm going to write my dreams," Adrianna said.

"I'm pretty good at English, so if you need me to proofread, I can help with that."

Alice took her homework out and put it in a stack next to her. She began to work on it while everyone else was talking around her. She listened as well, but she needed to wait until they stopped talking about that English assignment. She had arranged her homework stack so that English was at the bottom of the pile and she would not have to talk about what she might write. Luckily, there was only about a page of each subject to do, so Alice figured it would go quickly.

"Is Ms. Bilamora even going to read them?" Adrianna asked.

"Better safe, right?" Heather said.

"She won't read them," Robert said. "My brother had her.

She always assigns this and he said she never reads them. She just checks to make sure you wrote something on them and you get more marks the more full it is."

"So you can just write until the whole thing is full and it doesn't matter what it is?"

The conversation faded away as Alice got to work. It was clear they weren't going to stop talking about the assignment and she had nothing to contribute, so she should at least get her homework done. She hardly wanted to spend her whole weekend with it hanging over her head when she could actually have a whole weekend without anything that she had to do or anywhere she had to be. No doctor, no tutor, just a chance to do whatever she wanted.

The homework went by fairly easily. French was just a series of definitions. Personal Planning was a quiz about what she already knew about various personal subjects like puberty. She was part way through math before anyone noticed she wasn't any paying attention to them.

"God, Alice, how do you do that so fast?" Robert asked, peering over at her sheet of math problems. She was already half way through the sheet. "All this homework is going to take me all weekend!"

Alice blushed. "It's not that fast," Alice said. "It's just algebra. My tutor taught me this last year."

"And French!"

"It's just definitions…"

"Definitions in French!"

Heather looked at him like he'd just pointed out where the sky was. "Of course they're definitions in French. What else would they teach in French class?"

"Well, excuse me," Robert said. "We don't all come to school already fluent in French."

"Would you guys stop saying French so much?" Sarah asked. "Maybe we can do the math first?"

"But I suck at math!" Robert said. "Why are there letters in it now? It makes no sense."

"Maybe you should start paying attention in class," Kevin said.

"I do pay attention! Just not as much as Alice, apparently."

"Can you help me with the math?" Adrianna asked. "I don't get it with the letters, either."

Alice looked to her and then down at the sheet. She could feel her heart pounding and her head spinning a little. She forced herself to take a deep breath and tried to calm down. That was the bad thing about having friends, she realized. As much as she'd wanted them, she just didn't know how to handle it when they all paid attention to her at once.

"What are you having trouble with?" Alice asked, focusing on Adrianna. With just one person, she was okay.

"It's the letters," Adrianna said. "I mean, A is a letter, right? How is a letter also a number?"

"Pretend it's not a letter," Alice said. "It's like a puzzle and you're trying to figure out what it really is and it's just a number pretending to be a letter."

"Why would a number pretend to be a letter?"

Alice thought about it for a moment, but she didn't have an answer for that. She felt a surge of panic run through her, but took another deep breath, trying to think calmly to keep from panicking any more. "What if it were something else? Like a cake or a little bottle of something?"

"A cake?" Robert asked.

"Why a bottle?" Heather added.

Alice froze, realizing where the examples came from. She was thinking about Wonderland again.

"I need to go," Alice said quickly. She dumped her stuff into her bag quickly, scrambling to get it all in.

"What?" Kevin asked. "Why?"

"I just... I have to go," Alice said. She threw the bag over her shoulder and quickly made her way out of the common area. She could feel the eyes following her out and tried not to run, knowing that it would only draw more attention.

She knew she had to get away. That was her only thought and she clung to it, leaving the dorms and heading out into the rest of the campus. The day was still bright and young, with several people milling about the grounds. She tried to look normal as she walked away as quickly as she could. She didn't know where she was going, just picking a random direction and taking the path to wherever it would led her.

Wonderland. Why did she have to keep thinking about Wonderland? Why did the cat have to remind her?

She stopped at the pond on the campus grounds and took a seat against a tree overlooking the water. Not too many people made it out this far, most of them on the other side of the pond, and she was feeling a little calmer. Setting her bag down next to her, she pulled out the rest of her math home-work to finish it here, in the sunshine and with the still water to one side of her. It was calm, like the day she'd found that damn rabbit and fallen down the hole.

Out here with no one around, she let herself think about that day again. It was safe to think about Wonderland when there was no one around. It was a secret that she still knew that it had happened, but if anyone ever found that out, she would be sent back to the doctors again. She would rather forget the doctors than Wonderland.

It had been a nice day then, too. Alice couldn't remember what her sister had been reading that day, only that she wished it had pictures so that she could read too. And then the white rabbit had come along and she'd been dumb enough to follow him to Wonderland.

She finished the rest of her math without thinking much about it and tucked it back into her bag. She reached in for the last bit of homework, the small journal she'd written her name on and she opened it up to the first empty page. Just one page. She only had to write one page every day. This couldn't possibly be that hard.

Alice wanted to write about Wonderland. With the Cat's appearance, she couldn't quite get it out of her mind and she needed to get it out so that she could continue not talking about it and letting no one know that she was thinking about it again.

Maybe Ms. Bilamora really wouldn't read it.

"Hello, Alice."

Alice froze at the sound of the voice above her. She looked out to see the purple hair of another student hanging down from one of the low branches. He lifted his head up to stare at her with his purple eyes and smiled wider than he should have been able to.

"Hello Cat," she said carefully, looking around to make sure no one else could hear her. The few students that had been lingering had wandered back to campus, probably for dinner at this time. One couple was still on the other side of the pond, far enough away that they didn't seem to care what was happening. Comforted that they probably wouldn't be overheard, she straightened, her eyes meeting his. "What are you doing here?"

He looked at her quizzically a moment before answering. "I was perusing the inside of my mind," he said casually. "Or perhaps I was dreaming of the days when I was still a cat. It is nice to shed your skin now and then, however."

"You know what I mean," Alice told him.

"Meaning is so many things to so many different people," he began, dropping out of the tree and landing lightly on his feet. He towered over her, looking down with a toothy grin.

"I mean why are you here at Lucena Academy and not in… you know."

The Cheshire Cat, though he wasn't a cat at the moment, looked down at her and tilted his head. "Do you think I know the things in your mind?"

Alice got to her feet, dropping the book from her lap. "I mean why aren't you in Wonderland!" she snapped at him, but she tried to keep her voice down.

Cat seemed amused. "Tsk, tsk," he said again, waving a finger and bending down closer to her. "We are not to speak of such places here where things make sense and no one is mad but you and I. And you are trying so hard not to be mad. It would be a shame to ruin that."

"That doesn't answer my question," she said, taking a step back and bumping into the tree. She looked him over carefully, seeing that he was indeed in the Lucena Academy pants and short sleeved white collared shirt with the school emblem stitched into the front pocket. He even wore the tie and a watch on his wrist that didn't tick. "Do you go here?"

"Answers are not what will make you happy, but I suppose," he said, leaning in closer until his face was right in front of hers. "I have already told you, girl. Wonderland is not the land of fun and play that it was when you came all those clocks ago. It is no longer any of the things you like to so fondly remember. If you'd like to see the travesty, you will have to wait for your gift."

"The gift of going back to Wonderland?" she asked, her voice almost hopeful. Could she really go back?

"Ah!" Cat said, placing his finger on her lips. "We must not mention the land of the mad."

"But you already said it," she said, glaring at him and refusing to back away. Not that she could with the tree.

"Perhaps I did, perhaps I didn't," he said, his finger moving under her chin and tilting her head up to his. "And perhaps a cat holds enough tongues that he can't keep track of what he says any longer. It really is quite a difficult life, that of mine."

"Don't you think she's a little young for you?"

Alice looked away and saw one of Adrianna's brothers

coming closer. It was one of the triplets, though she wasn't entirely certain which one it was. Mike, Mark, and Matt were identical. This one, however, was alone rather than with his brothers and looked mad as he approached.

Cat growled and Alice looked back at him.

"My dear," he said, backing away. "You will see everything you wish when you turn twelve and a half. You celebrated the day once. We will celebrate it again and you will learn to hold your tongue where I will not catch it."

He turned and left, wandering off without even a glance back or a wave. Alice watched him go, her mind turning. Wonderland. Could he really bring her back to Wonderland? She'd spent so much time trying to convince people she'd really gone, without luck. Maybe if she went this time, she could bring back proof that it was real. Or maybe she would learn that the doctors were right and she had imagined it all.

Adrianna's brother came up to her. "Are you okay?" he asked.

"What?" Alice asked, looking at him. She could almost see the Hatter in his face and realized that she was going to have trouble talking to anyone right now without slipping in a reference to Wonderland. "I'm fine."

"You know that guy?"

"I have to go," she said, picking up her bag. "Sorry, I have to go."

She left in a jog, her thoughts on getting away. She didn't pay attention to where she was going, only that she needed to get away. She slowed down once she hit the concrete of a path and she noticed her bag was unzipped at the top. She closed it and kept moving forward, not sure where she was going or even where she was, letting her mind wander now that she was alone again.

She once dreamed every night about going back to Wonderland. As scary as some of it was, and how annoying some of the other inhabitants were, there was so much there that she wanted to see. It was like she'd stepped into one of the story books Lori used to read to her and, now that she'd been once, she thought she could handle it better.

The Cheshire Cat had gotten out and even become human. He was a student at Lucena Academy, though she couldn't imagine him attending classes. He probably did know a way back and she couldn't think of a time he'd lied to her before.

That, of course, being part of the problem. He said there was trouble in Wonderland now. She didn't know what happened, but it worried her more than she felt it should. She hadn't even been there in years and didn't think she'd ever get to go back, but the thought that something was wrong there made her stomach clench.

Alice looked around and realized that she didn't know where she was. She was by a building with vines growing up the side with a garden leading into the forest on the other side. The path she was on ended, but there was a small side door a few steps behind her.

It opened when she tried it and she went inside, finding herself in a strange room with all sorts of costumes. It smelled musty, like it needed the door left open, but she left it as it was, looking without touching and marvelling at the costumes and props. They were medieval and modern and futuristic and all sorts of things that she had never seen before.

The room was like a labyrinth, but she gradually made her way through until she found another door leading to something a little more familiar. The black cloth draped from the high ceiling to the floor and the catwalk high above her was a good hint, anyway. A soft light came from the other side of the curtains and she made her way out onto the stage, recognizing this place at last.

She knew she should head back to the dorms, or at least to dinner, but her mind was still spinning. Wonderland. She had so many questions and so many things she needed to know. And she might be able to go back.

She hopped off the stage and out into the lobby, wandering around until she found the stairs again. No one was here, thankfully, to ask her what she was doing. Alone, she made her way up and took a seat in one of the windows from before that overlooked the rooftop garden. The vines probably grew down from here, not the other way around, she realized.

What was she going to do? She was never going to stop thinking about Wonderland now. No matter how hard she would try to not talk about it, it was going to slip and she'd be sent home. Her father would be furious and send her back to the doctors again. She'd already slipped once today and that was without thinking about how she might be able to go back at last.

She started going through her bag, looking for her English journal. Maybe she could just tell Ms. Bilamora that it was a story and she would never mention it to her parents. She would turn in so many other fantastic assignments the rest of the year and her journal would be completely forgotten.

Or she would find another notebook. She'd make the money somehow to buy another one from the school store and she would write everything in there. Either way, she needed to get all of her thoughts about Wonderland out of her head.

The book wasn't in her bag. She emptied it out on the ledge, but she couldn't find the journal anywhere. Hoping that she wouldn't fail just because she lost the book, she went back through everything she'd done since getting it that afternoon to see where it had gone as she packed her bag. She had it when she went for homework with Adrianna. She had it under the tree. It was on her lap until...

"Stupid Cat!" she yelled, throwing her bag back down to the ground beside her. Everything kept leading back to him. He made her think about Wonderland, made her think that she might even get to go back, and now she'd made him lose her journal for class.

"Alice?"

Alice looked up and around for the voice. "Hello?" she called back.

Coming up the stairs was one of Adrianna's brothers, one of the triplets. "There you are," he said, smiling and holding her journal in his hand. "You dropped this. Ms. Bilamora's class, right?"

He brought it up the stairs and handed it to her, Alice not really sure how to respond. "Thank you," she said. Nothing to make anyone think she was talking about Wonderland with that. It was polite and she was grateful. "Where did you find it?"

"You dropped it when you ran off," he said. "Are you okay?"

"I'm fine," she said, her eyes going down to the book and flipping through it. The pages were blank, but at least she had something to look at other than him.

"He wasn't bugging you, was he?"

"No."

"Do you know who he is?"

Alice opened her mouth to reply but stopped. If she said yes, she might have to explain why and she didn't have an explanation for that yet. When else would she have met him? He obviously went to the high school and the only people she knew in the high school were Adrianna's brothers.

"I didn't think he even went here," he continued, taking a seat on the window sill with Alice. "He just sleeps in that tree. And I know you aren't allowed to dye your hair like that. It's like he just stole a uniform so he could sneak onto campus and sleep."

Alice stayed quiet, absorbed in her empty journal. If she said nothing, maybe he would go away and she could write enough about Wonderland in the journal that she wouldn't feel tempted to slip something about it into conversation.

"You know him," he said.

He wasn't going away. Alice thought as quickly as she could to find a way to divert the conversation. "I'm sorry, which one are you?" she asked. "You three look a lot alike."

He smiled, mischief in his eyes. "Matt," he said, though Alice could tell he was lying.

"Your brothers are up to something, aren't they?"

"I'm afraid I don't know what you're talking about," he said. "But it is lovely to have someone to talk to who can assure everyone that, I, Matt, was nowhere near the dorms and had absolutely nothing to do with it."

"Matt." Alice smiled back at him. She'd have to ask Adrianna why he was lying later.

"Now, how do you know that guy?" he asked quickly, as if trying to trick her into an answer.

Alice hesitated, trying to figure out a response that was devoid of anything Wonderland related, but she could possibly repeat in the future if she was asked again. "An old acquaintance," she said. "Cat's an old acquaintance."

"His name's Cat?"

Alice's eyes snapped back down at her journal, but he didn't seem bothered by it.

"And he knows when your half birthday is. I think he's got a thing for you."

A thing where he wants to drive me insane, Alice thought.

Matt looked outside, the sun setting over the garden of the roof. "I think they should be done by now," he said, getting to his feet. "Let's go?"

Alice hesitated. "I think I'm going to finish this," she said, indicating the journal. He left without asking anything else, leaving her to her book.

She opened it and took out a pencil. Much longer and she might have said something about Wonderland. Why did he have to keep talking about that cat? She opened up to the first page, her stomach rumbling but her mind determined. She needed to get at least some of it out before she was around people again or she'd say something.

She started writing about that first day by the bank with her sister. From the beginning, she decided. She would write everything from the beginning.

CHAPTER 3

Dinner Party

"DID YOU HEAR what they did this time?" Sarah asked as they worked on their homework.

Alice kept her head down, working out the last pieces of her homework. Adrianna's brothers started the year by somehow changing all the locks on all the doors in the dorms while Matt was talking to Alice and everyone else was getting dinner.

It was a spectacular opening that was easily remedied by everyone switching keys, and the three of them getting off because Alice had been talking to Matt, who all three of them claimed to be. While Evan was eventually brought in to tell them apart, Alice couldn't identify which brother she'd been talking to. In the end, they all got detention, but were not punished nearly as harshly as she imagined they could have been.

The detention hadn't stopped them, instead provided them an alibi when more things started going wrong. It was never anything that caused permanent damage or couldn't be easily fixed. Food was dyed, things went missing for a day, but it was never anything harmful. They seemed to know what the limits were.

Alice was just glad she could no longer be used as an alibi again. After the first time, Adrianna had taught her the differences between the three of them. The one she'd been talking to was Mike, who sometimes had to squint to see things because he refused to wear his glasses. Mark's voice was ever so slightly lower than his brothers' and Matt had a mole in the middle of his left palm. They were small differences, but it was enough that she was no longer a reliable alibi.

Adrianna didn't say much when her brothers came up in conversation either. She didn't say much at all when they were doing homework, Alice noticed. While everyone else talked and worked on things, Adrianna always seemed to struggle to figure out everything on the page. When her brothers came up, Alice made a habit of leaning over and seeing if she needed help.

"How's yours?" she asked.

"I don't get it," she said quietly. "Which numbers go with which letters?"

Alice leaned over and started to help her figure out which

letters replaced what, still amazed at her roommate. Adrianna was nice, good with vocabulary in other languages and memorizing formulas, but she could never figure out how to put anything together. Alice was patient and able to show her, though waited until everyone else was too distracted to notice her doing it.

"Thanks," Adrianna said as she got through a few questions. "You think you can help with the rest later tonight?"

"Why not now?" Alice asked.

"I'm supposed to meet my brothers for dinner," she said, smiling. "Oh, they wanted you to come too!"

"Don't your brothers see you, like, all the time?" Heather asked, overhearing them and chiming in.

"Oh, not those ones," Adrianna told her.

"You have *more*?" Robert asked.

Adrianna nodded. "My older ones. Evan, Joe, and Travis go to the high school. They wanted to check in on me. Apparently they've been seeing lots of Mike and Mark and Matt."

"I bet," Kevin said with a bit of a smile.

"Do you have any more than that?" Robert demanded.

"Well, Ryan," she said. "But he's in university now, so he's not coming."

Robert's head hit the table.

"Can't you leave Alice?" Sarah asked. "She's the only one who gets this math stuff."

"You just have to replace the letters with numbers and solve for the last number," Alice said, not looking at anyone. "You guys can figure it out."

"It's okay, Alice," Kevin said. "I get it. I'll help them."

"Thanks."

Adrianna and Alice excused themselves and went back up to their room to drop off their homework. They'd both settled into their room pretty well, Alice unpacking all of her things into her wardrobe and drawers. Her desk stayed fairly bare, rarely using it since most of her homework was done while she was with everyone else. The only thing she worked on was her English journal, well away from anyone else who might look over her shoulder.

She never had to worry about Adrianna reading it. She was usually working on revising her homework in the evenings and played music for them to listen to while they worked. At night, they talked about the day and Alice felt like she'd really made a friend here.

"Should I know anything about these brothers?" Alice asked, taking her English journal out and putting it on her desk. She already knew about them, but she thought she knew about the triplets too until they tried to turn her into an alibi.

"Not really," she said. "Evan's meeting us in the student council room."

"You know where that is, right?"

Adrianna nodded, smiling as she led the way out and over to the clubs building between the middle and high school buildings. "It's okay. They're really nice. And you already met Evan, so Travis and Joe will be super easy."

"They don't like pranks, do they? I'm not going to need some way to tell them apart?"

"No. Joe and Travis never wanted anyone to mix them up so they decided to be really different from each other. You'll be fine."

Alice nodded, but wasn't really sure what she was in for. She wished Adrianna had mentioned something earlier, but she didn't know what she might have done differently. Tried to get out of it? And Adrianna's brothers had been nice enough so far. At least Evan had, and even the triplets were nice when they weren't up to something.

They made it up to the student council room, which was just a large room on the top floor with a view of the rest of the campus outside of the picture window. There were things written on white boards, a few computers scattered about and a long table in the middle to sit at where there were already two people hanging out. They were laughing when Alice and Adrianna entered.

"Addie!" one of them said, both of them looking over to her. "You made it! And this is Alice?"

"Yep!" Adrianna said. "Alice, this is Joe and Travis."

"Hi," Alice said, smiling and looking between them both. If not for their faces, she would have never guessed that they were twins at all.

Travis had his light brown hair cut short and just seemed wider. He was more tanned, too, and one of his teeth had a small chip in it that she could see when he smiled.

Joe was slimmer and pale by comparison. He dyed his hair black and let it grow as long as school regulation would allow it. He smiled too, but he didn't show his teeth like Travis did.

"We've been wanting to meet this roommate," Joe said, looking at Travis. "Good of you to join us."

Alice wasn't really sure what to say to that, though took a seat with Adrianna when she did. "How've you been?" Joe asked Adrianna. "Homesick?"

Adrianna shook her head no as Evan came in, carrying a picnic's worth of food. Alice greeted him along with everyone else and took her share as the conversation turned to retelling stories of their first semester. Adrianna lead, but kept asking Alice to add in what she could.

Alice found herself comfortable around them. They didn't interrupt or interrogate her, and even when she talked about how often she got lost they didn't laugh at her. Instead, they offered their own stories of getting lost and how they found certain places in the school from doing that. It was fun, strangely, and Alice couldn't even remember why she'd been so nervous.

Adrianna was telling Evan about how tough homework was here when Travis leaned in to talk to Alice. "So Alice," Travis said as the light outside started to fade, "do you know Lori Liddell?"

"She's my sister," Alice said.

"What happened to her?" he asked. "She was in our class, but she hasn't been back this year."

Alice shrugged. "She just kind of left for London one day," Alice said. "It was weird. I was out with my tutor and when I came back, mom said she was off to London and she was going to be going to school there for a while. She didn't even say goodbye."

"That's..." Travis said, though he looked at a loss for words.

"So that's what happened," Joe said, his eyes on Travis. Their eyes met, but Alice didn't know what passed between them. "She was a friend of ours," Joe said to Alice. "We were a little worried when she didn't show up and we didn't hear from her. So you don't know what happened?"

Alice shook her head. "My parents didn't tell me. They said that I didn't really need to know." She shrunk under Travis' gaze. He looked so sad for her and she didn't know why. "It's okay," she tried to assure him. "They don't usually tell me anything more than I need to know. They want me to focus on my studies."

"It sounds like you're doing pretty well in that area," Joe said.

"Alice is so smart!" Adrianna chimed in. "I don't get any of this stuff, but she's been trying to help me."

"You'll get it," Alice told Adrianna.

"I hear you know our mystery student too," Evan said, looking to Alice.

"Who?" Travis asked.

"The kid with the purple hair," Joe said. "Sleeps in that tree by the pond. Never goes to class, no one knows who he is and no one can seem to catch him or figure out what he's doing on campus."

"You know him?"

Alice shrunk a little at the question. "He's an old acquaintance," she said, remembering her answer from before. When no one said anything, she knew they were waiting for more details. "His name is Cat," she offered.

"Mike said something about him giving you a gift on your half birthday," Evan said. "Is this guy giving you trouble?"

Alice shook her head. "I haven't even seen him since then," she said. It was true, though it was largely because she had purposely avoided going back to the pond. He hadn't sought her out either, mercifully.

"Do people still celebrate half birthdays?" Travis asked.

"We used to when we were little," Joe reminded him. "Tried to have a party and everything, but the boys had their birthday."

"Oh yeah."

"When's your half birthday?" Joe asked Alice.

Alice thought about it for a minute, counting months on her fingers. "November 4th."

"So tomorrow. Happy half birthday." He smiled at her and she laughed, though she could feel something shift in the room. "You and Addie should do something to celebrate."

"Like what?"

"Try playing a prank on the boys," Joe suggested. "They really need a taste of their own medicine."

That garnered a laugh. They devolved into ideas to prank the triplets with, each more outlandish than the last, until Evan finally declared it too late for the girls to be out of their dorms. Even with the weekend, he thought it was getting late and he walked the two of them back to their dorm at the end of the night.

They went back to their room, Adrianna getting ready for bed while Alice went to her desk.

"You aren't tired?"

"A little," Alice said. "I'm almost done, though."

"Done? Like, the whole book?" Adrianna was amazed, looking past Alice to the journal on her desk. "How?"

"Inspired, I guess," Alice said.

"What are you writing about?"

Alice hesitated. Adrianna asked once in a while and she never really had an answer for her. "You know," she said. "Stuff."

"I wish I could think of as much stuff as you," Adrianna said. "Good night."

"Night," Alice said, turning the lamp on her desk on as Adrianna turned the rest of the lights off and she went to bed. Alice opened up her journal and got to work.

It was almost full, but she was almost done. The book held all of her adventures in Wonderland, starting from the day with her sister when she followed the white rabbit. It was cathartic in a way to go back through everything. It had been years since she was allowed to go through the entire story again and now, with it all written down, she found herself no longer tempted to talk about it anymore because she could come back to the book and relive it.

Not that she wanted to relive much of it. Crying so many tears she nearly drowned in them wasn't fun, nor was growing into the White Rabbit's house or when the Queen of Hearts put her on trial and tried to remove her head. Other parts weren't as bad, granted, and the Caterpillar had been nice if a little odd. Even the Hatter and the Hare weren't that bad, though she knew better than to have tea with them again.

She finished the rest of the story of the trial now, and when the cards swarmed over her. She didn't quite know what was going on, but she was defiant back then. Her sister woke her from somewhere along the shore, looking surprised to see her and confiding in her later that she'd been looking for Alice for hours.

While she wanted to start writing about what happened after with the doctors, she was out of pages before she even had a chance to say that Lori never really quite knew if she would believe her. There were only three lines left in her journal and she had so much still to say.

It was enough for now, though. She never wanted to talk about the doctors in the same way that she wanted to talk about Wonderland. Wonderland she wanted to remember, but the doctors she would rather put behind her forever.

She went to bed, feeling better now that she had gotten it all out. The writing and the memories exhausted her. She crawled into bed without bothering to change out of her uniform and curling up under the covers. Sleep came quickly.

CHAPTER 4

Falling

THE WEIGHT ON her bed woke her up a few hours later. She wasn't normally such a light sleeper but this time, something about the weight seemed incredibly out of place. It was like their cat, Dinah, was here, sitting on her chest and getting ready to paw at her face until she woke up to feed her. Except that Dinah ran away years ago.

When she opened her eyes, there were purple ones staring back at her. She gasped and suppressed the urge to scream. The cat pulled back and smiled a wide, toothy grin. "Good to have you awake," he said. "Come along, we don't have all night. Well, we do, really, but that's what they say in places like these, where time is something that people believe rules them and not the other way around."

"Cat?" she asked, wiping at her sleep-filled eyes and letting out a long yawn. It took her a moment to realize he was here, now in a more familiar purple tabby. When she spoke again, her voice was a harsh whisper and her eyes were darting back and forth between him and the sleeping Adrianna. "What are you doing here? And at this hour?"

"This hour, that hour," he said, not bothering to keep his voice down. "I am here to wish you a delightful half birthday, Alice my dear, and you would have this day forgot all together."

"Because most people don't celebrate their half birthday," Alice said. "Now leave or I'll call Miss Amanda. She'll kick you out herself so I can get some sleep."

"What difference is sleep now than sleep any other time?" he asked. "Now that you are awake, come for a walk. There are few people here who would enjoy the experience of being lost quite like you would and I should very much like to get lost. I have quite good direction, however, and will need a guide."

"You aren't going to go away and let me sleep, are you?" Alice asked, staring at him and wishing that he would drop through the floor and reveal that he was nothing more than a dream. She pinched the inside of her wrist, just to be sure. He, however, continued to smile back at her. "I'll get in trouble if I go with you," she insisted, though she found herself already putting her shoes back on.

"Do dress nicely," Cat said, moving to the door. "You

never know what wonders might be out there and when someone might be offended that you were not ready to meet them."

Cat stepped out the door. Alice thought about going
back to sleep. No, she should follow him. If she didn't, she'd
always wonder what would have happened and she would
be thinking about Wonderland all the time. If she went,
she might be able to just write it out again. It wouldn't be
long. If it was like last time, she would be back before Adrianna woke up and she could dismiss the whole thing as a
dream.

She grabbed a black headband to keep her hair from falling in her face and went out the door to find Cat standing
immediately behind her. "I suppose," he said, slipping around
her to take the lead, "that I should pay you some gratitude.
You have given me a name, which I never needed before I
came here to this mad, or not so mad, world. It has seemed to
make things easier for me."

"Are you sure we aren't going to get caught?" Alice asked,
falling into step behind him. She kept looking around for
any movement.

"Is that what I said?" Cat asked. "I do not recall. There are
so many things I say these days. How can I possibly remember
them all?"

Alice's heart sank, but they were already stepping out of
the dorms. She continued to look around and jump at the

shadows, fearful that she would be caught out of bed after hours, but determined to see Wonderland again.

"Where are we going?" Alice asked finally, Cat having slowed his pace in the cool night air to enjoy looking at the stars. She looked up too, but found that, while they were lovely, she couldn't quite bring herself to enjoy them.

"We are going to get lost," he said with a smile on his face. "You are quite good at that and you shall be my guide. There will be an adventure as your reward, my gratitude repaid in proper kind. An adventure for me and one for you as well."

"We're going to get caught and I'm the only one going to get in trouble for it because I'm the only one who actually goes to this school," she said.

"So worried," he said. "You used to enjoy the journey. I hoped you would still."

She didn't say anything for a while, turning the words over and over again in her mind. There was something more happening here, but she didn't know what it was. There was something wrong here.

"Tell me about Wonderland," she said finally, watching him for some reaction. His ears drooped and his tail sagged, a sign of sadness.

"Wonderland," he said as they passed through an archway into the high school campus, moving slower and Alice unwittingly taking the lead again. Alice opened the door, watching Cat, and led the way inside.

If Alice weren't so worried about getting caught, she might have wondered why the door was unlocked.

"Wonderland has changed. It is no longer fun and games and tea."

It hadn't really been all fun and games when she was there either, though Alice thought it best not to remind him. The Queen of Hearts had attempted to behead her when she was there, if she remembered right. She was pretty sure that she did.

"Something has entered Wonderland," he said at last. "Something that let you in, it let other things in which were not so much fun to play with. We were hospitable, but Wonderland has become a different sort of game now."

"What sort of game?" Alice asked. "When I was there, the game involved my head being removed from my shoulders."

He let out a sigh and slunk around to the lead again, grinning. "Now, are we quite lost yet? I would quite like to have this adventure begin."

Alice stopped at the top of the stairs and was certain this wasn't where she had been a moment ago. "Yes," she said. "Yes, we are now lost."

"Good," Cat said. "Now, all we have to do is become found again."

Alice tensed. Being found was not something she wanted to do. She was not supposed to be out of bed at this hour and she was certainly not supposed to be wandering around the high school.

He led the way, which Alice presumed was probably for the best. He said he had a good sense of direction and, so long as he didn't do anything to get them found, then perhaps he could find the way.

"What happened to Wonderland?" she asked again. They were going through classrooms and up stairs that she was sure weren't supposed to be there, but she was trying to stay calm. The school wasn't supposed to be like this. She pinched the inside of her wrist hard, but she didn't wake up. This was real, but this wasn't normal.

The cat slowly disappeared much like he used to. He left Alice there for a moment, his grin the last thing to fade away until the door at the top of the steps opened. "Come along, Alice."

Alice looked back down the stairs, but there was only darkness there. She ran up the stairs, trying to keep calm despite wanting to panic. "Don't just run from me!" she called after him, trying to focus on something else. "What happened?"

She ran up the stairs and found herself face to face with a mirror, the Cat slinking around from behind her, startling her with his breath on her ear. "You want to know what happened to Wonderland?" he asked. "You can find out for yourself. You don't like pretending not to be mad in a world of a different kind of madness. We liked you, Alice. You were mad. We were mad. We had tea."

Cat grinned wide. Alice looked at him, but she didn't know how to respond anymore and he disappeared behind her. She looked in the mirror and saw herself there, in a land with flowers with mouths that were chatting. It was Wonderland, looking bright and more vibrant than anything here. Wonderland.

She turned back to say something to him, but he was under her feet. She tried to pull her feet out from amidst him curling around them, but lost her balance and fell through the mirror.

CHAPTER 5

The Dormouse's Tale

ALICE LANDED HARD in the dirt in the middle of the day. The sun was high in the sky, beaming down pleasantly. She got to her feet and brushed off her uniform, taking a look around. She was in the garden, though it wasn't quite as bright and vibrant as it looked in the mirror. Instead, it was a sea of green stems with very few flowers on the ends of them.

She spotted two of them a little further down from where she was. They had faces and were already chatting with one another about the tragedy of what had happened and how they were the only two left.

Alice walked the other way to avoid them.

She kept pinching the inside of her wrist hard, but she wasn't waking up. It was all really here, real as she was.

Wonderland. She knew it was Wonderland. She felt a surge of panic, but made herself keep walking. Her father would be so mad if he found out. She'd be sent back to the doctors and she would probably never get to see the sun again.

When Alice came back from Wonderland the last time, her parents had only tolerated her tales of Wonderland for a month before telling her that she had dreamed it all. It didn't matter that Lori had been looking for her for hours and couldn't find her. They were convinced that Alice was making it all up. Some point after that, they realized that she wasn't, and instead started taking her to see doctors.

Alice was taken out of school when she continued telling her friends about Wonderland. She was homeschooled and not allowed to see anyone until they all forgot she was there. Instead, she saw doctors who told her it was all in her head and gave her pills that made it hard to think. They told her to pinch herself whenever something that reminded her of Wonderland happened, just to remind herself that it wasn't real. They told her that she was lying and that she was mad.

She agreed with them once. Slowly, she learned that if she continued to agree with them, then they would start to think she was better.

Lori helped her. Her older sister taught her how to lie and look people in the eyes when you did it. She taught Alice to create a version of the world that she could pretend was real — the version that the doctors and her parents wanted to be real — and how to make them believe that she believed it too.

Alice took a deep breath. She could do it. Once she got back, she could continue to pretend that none of this had ever happened. So long as she never told anyone, she wouldn't be sent back. And she knew she could keep a secret.

Besides, she had been sent by the Cheshire Cat to do something. Something was wrong in Wonderland and she was supposed to do...

She didn't know what she was supposed to do while she was here, actually. Wonderland did feel strange, though. The air was colder, the flowers decapitated and the colours a little less vibrant than she remembered. But the flowers talked and she could feel the nonsense and madness in the air.

She found a path to follow into the hills and decided to take it. She needed to find out what was wrong with Wonderland. Something about this path seemed familiar and she hoped it would bring her to someone she remembered that might actually help her instead of talking in circles. If Wonderland wanted her help, it would need to start being nicer to her.

And then she saw it. That table off in the distance and the shine off of what was probably the broken clock. There was a tea party waiting for her. She continued walking, mentally preparing for irritating conversation and determined to make the Hatter be clear this time.

As she drew nearer and nearer, she knew something was

different. There was no joy. The table wasn't the bustle it was last time. Alice suspected that had something to do with the clock. It was no longer stuck at six o'clock and keeping the occupants of the table in perpetual tea time and switching seats just as they were about to take a bite or a sip of tea. Instead, the clock was smashed and in pieces on the ground, springs coming out of its face and nothing in it looking like it was going to be able to keep anyone anywhere.

The Hatter, she saw as she came closer, was pacing around, pouring cups of tea as and absently sipping at them as he went, looking back and forth from the table to the clock, then back to the table again, sipping and pouring. Many of the cups were overflowing. The pot was empty. The Hatter didn't even seem to notice that Alice was standing there watching.

He looked completely dishevelled and like he might actually make some sense. He reminded her of the days when her father had a difficult day at work and she would have to be careful to stay out of sight until he felt a little better.

Though he usually got better with a cup of tea. The Hatter seemed to have no shortage of that.

"Pardon me," Alice said, careful with her manners this time. The Hatter turned around, a spark of hope in his eyes dying once he laid eyes on Alice. He held her gaze, though looked somewhat disappointed that she wasn't someone else. "Are you all right?"

He seemed to come back to himself a little at that one, straightening up and adjusting his hat so it was properly on his head once more. "Well, lacking just as much civility as you always have been, I see!" He came up close to inspect her. "You do look awfully familiar, anyway. And if you do look familiar, then I daresay I might have known you once."

"You may have indeed," Alice said. He seemed to be recovering. "I attended a tea party with you here once. Although attended might be the wrong word. I didn't actually get to drink any tea the last time I was here."

"Ah, then you must have been doing something wrong then," the Hatter said, escorting her to the table. "Please, do take a seat. Dormouse, wake up you lazy thing, we have a guest!"

"Ah, has he returned then?" the mouse said, though he didn't seem to actually have woken up at all. He was sleeping in the sugar bowl.

"Oh no," the Hatter said, looking a little nervous. "Not yet. He will be along, though. Yes, he'll be along very soon."

"Who will be?" Alice asked.

"The March Hare, of course," the Hatter said, continuing to look back and forth at the clock again, as if the smashed clock might make him appear. "The March Hare must have just gotten lost on his way back. Silly thing, can never remember where he is or what he's meant to be doing, making the rest of us worry."

Alice nodded and didn't say anything. She was feeling thirsty and, while the tea was probably cold, she could use a drink of something. She brought the cup to her lips.

The cold tea touched her lips and she jerked the cold liquid away. She dropped the cup back down onto the saucer and pushed herself away from the table. No. She wasn't going to drink anything. No food, no drink. Last time, everything made her change shape. She wouldn't be doing that again.

She shifted her attention to the table and realized that there were vines starting to grow amidst the tea party, like the trees were going to try and take over the grove now that time was destroyed, and there was nothing else keeping them here. The more she looked around, the more she noticed the decay that the place had fallen into. The flowers were nowhere near as vibrant as the last time. Alice was almost certain that the pastries and butter were from the last time she was here, too.

"Excuse me," Alice said quietly to the Dormouse. He did say before that he heard everything, even if he was sleeping more often than he was awake. "How long has the Hatter been waiting for the Hare to return?" she asked.

The mouse muttered something in his sleep before letting out a sigh. "Oh," he said, though it sounded almost like he were breathing out rather than actually speaking. "Several months now."

"Has he been like this since?"

"Yes, indeed he has," the Dormouse said. He paused a moment before saying, "I'm not asleep, you know. Just resting my eyes."

"You're always asleep," the Hatter said, coming back along to this side of the table until he was right next to Alice. "I don't suppose you know what happens when you try to play chess with a deck of cards?"

"No, I'm afraid not," Alice said, trying to at least be polite.

"Oh," he said, looking a little disappointed. "Shame that. It is a good thing to know these days. Dangerous place, Wonderland has become. No place for a young person or plant or hare to be wandering about all alone. What did you say your name was, dear?"

Alice was a little taken aback at the term of endearment at the end. *Dear*. It sounded out of place coming from him. "Alice," she said. "I'm Alice. It's interesting to be back here again."

"I should say so," the Mad Hatter agreed. "We heard that you went to see the Queen of Hearts. Well, that you'd seen her before —" his hand rolled in the air "— well, everyone knows what happened."

"I'm afraid I don't know," Alice said, trying to think of a

way to keep this momentum. She needed to know what happened and the Mad Hatter seemed to know not only what was going on, but his eyes lit up, excited and appalled at the idea that anyone wouldn't know.

"The Dormouse shall tell us the story!" the Hatter proclaimed, stepping over and pinching him on one side. The Dormouse rolled out of the cup of sugar, which seemed to have knocked some sense into him. "Wake up, you silly thing," the Hatter said. "We wish for a story and have decided you will tell it."

"Oh, it's all right," Alice said, remembering the tale of the treacle. A treacle well and pictures of muchness had driven her mad trying to understand the last time she was here and she was certain that she didn't want to endure another tale like that. "I don't need to hear a story. I'm sure Dormouse would be much happier going back to sleep than telling a story, really, wouldn't you?"

"Do you not like stories?" the Dormouse asked, sounding offended.

"Oh, I like stories!" Alice said, trying to sound earnest. "It's just, you seem so tired and I wouldn't want to trouble you with one. And the Mad Hatter was just—"

"I'm not asleep, you know," the Dormouse informed her. "I am fully able to tell a story."

"Oh," Alice said. "I didn't mean to say you were. I'm sorry."

Neither the Dormouse, nor the Hatter seemed to notice the dread in her voice and the quiet plea that he should simply go back to sleep. He looked back and forth, but the Hatter wasn't really paying that much attention, more content with topping off the cups with an empty tea pot.

Alice slumped onto the table, resting her chin in her palm. She would endure whatever story the Dormouse had for her and then go back to trying to get something out of the Hatter.

"Once upon a time," the Dormouse began, "there was the Queen of Hearts. She was a strange woman who kept demanding people be beheaded for doing nothing more than possibly one day committing a crime. It helped quite a bit, none of those people ever getting a chance to commit a crime, but it was a terrible thing all together, really."

Alice straightened, puzzled. Was he really going to be telling a story that made some sort of sense? Maybe this was the change to Wonderland that Cat talked about. Maybe it meant that Wonderland was going to start making some sense and the madness would finally start to subside.

"No one's head really ever came off, though. Not often, anyway. The King of Hearts quietly pardoned everyone until one day he died. A sad thing, really."

"When did the King of Hearts die?" Alice asked.

"One day," the Dormouse repeated. "I said that. You should really listen."

Nope. The madness was still there.

"The Queen was quite distraught and didn't know what she was going to do. Not right away, anyway. You need to spend a little bit of time not knowing what to do, you see, because it's proper manners and the Queen had to follow those."

"I don't remember her having many manners when I met her," Alice muttered.

"Shush!" the Hatter snapped at her and Alice fell silent again.

"Then she started to do something terrible. All of her men had lost their hearts. The Queen had stolen them. She had decided that everyone must give her their hearts now instead of their heads and she started to go about, demanding 'Out with their Hearts!' instead. This time the King of Hearts wasn't there to stop her from doing it anymore."

"She's been killing people?" Alice asked, horrified.

"No," the Hatter said, looking at her like she asked which direction the sky was. "That would be barbaric! Completely unbefitting of a Queen! She's only been taking their hearts."

"But you can't live without your heart."

"Of course you can!" The Hatter told her. "There are

heartless people everywhere. Now be civil and let Dormouse continue the story."

Alice went quiet.

The Dormouse was snoring lightly.

"Oh, wake up!" the Hatter snapped at him, pinching his nose until he sneezed.

The mouse awoke, looking up at both of them. "I wasn't asleep," he said. "Just resting my eyes. Now, where was I?"

"You were saying how the Queen demanded hearts instead of heads," Alice said.

"Yes, indeed she was," the Dormouse nodded. "But it wasn't her turn to be Queen anymore. The White King and the Red King were using Wonderland to determine which of them would be in charge next, but the Queen of Hearts wouldn't step down anymore. She was quite mad, really, that the Red King mistook her for his wife. She took his heart and the Red Queen went missing after that. Terrible thing. Then she found the White Queen and got rid of her and ensured they wouldn't ever beat her in another game again. Sentencing before they committed any crime. Quite a successful a strategy, really."

"That sounds terrible!"

"Not really," the Dormouse said. "It worked. That's all that really counts. Right?"

"Not really."

The Dormouse yawned before going on. "When the Red King went to the Queen of Hearts, thinking she was his wife, the White King sent for his messengers. He needs two, you see, and they were both here. There needs to be one to come and one to go. The March Hare was to come and our dear Mad Hatter is the one that is meant to go. When they wanted the two of them to start performing their duties again, the White Knight destroyed the clock and tea time ended."

"It was a bit of a sad thing," the Hatter said. "I did quite like the tea. But one has a duty to their king and when we were called the March Hare came and I waited for my orders to go."

Alice wasn't sure that made any sense, but this was Wonderland.

"He's been waiting for quite a while now," the Dormouse said; his little tired voice almost sad. "Since then, the cards have been moving around with the Queen and stealing hearts. The White King is trying awfully hard to do something, but he's lost quite a few of his own men and he's not able to move as much as he'd like to. But he must not fall or all is lost."

"It sounds like things are serious," Alice said. "Are you sure the March Hare didn't get in trouble with the Queen of Hearts?"

"I've been given no news," the Hatter said. He straightened himself up and fixed his coat again, trying to look like he didn't care. "It's probably because nothing that important has been found yet. The March Hare will come when they find something. I am a messenger for the White King, and he is the only King that remains since the Queen of Hearts tricked the Red King. Nasty woman that."

The Hatter shook his head and started to pace about the table again, pouring from the empty pot into already full cups.

"That silly Hare has gone and forgotten what he was meant to do, so he's taken a nap and gotten himself lost. He's really quite rubbish at the job, you know," he explained to Alice. "He tries, oh sure, but it's not terribly useful when he can't remember where he's going or what he's doing most of the time. A real shame, but the White King, bless his heart, he wanted to do something to make him quite useful."

The Hatter sighed and sat back into one of the seats, looking somewhat disappointed. "Ah, but that means that I cannot do my duty for the White King yet then," he sighed. "Not until that damned Hare does his. The White King cannot send a message out that he hasn't received yet, you see. Hrm, now I do wonder if he even remembered to bring the message with him at all," the Hatter pondered, raising the edge of the tablecloth from their table up and going under it.

"What are you looking for?" Alice asked, looking under the table, but it seemed that the Mad Hatter was no longer under there when she looked. She sat back up and the Hatter was there with a pie in hand that promptly fell onto Alice's face.

She didn't move, though the Hatter looked quite upset. "Now why did you go and do a thing like that?" he asked. "That was hardly very civil of you. That pie was for the White King."

Alice was glad the pie covered the anger on her face. She took a moment to breathe in through the pie, but it was not easy. She wiped it off her face, some of it ending up in her mouth and she swallowed the largely tasteless filling. She saw the Hatter, looking horrified that she had done such a thing and lost her temper.

"I didn't do anything!" she yelled at him. "You dropped it on me! What kind of pie is this? Is it going to make me shrink or grow this time?"

"It's an unbirthday pie," the Hatter said as if it were the most obvious thing in the world. "It was supposed to be what March Hare was supposed to bring to the White King."

"What's an unbirthday?" Alice asked, confused. "Do you mean his birthday?"

"Oh no," the Hatter said, laughing. "You only have one birthday a year, but your unbirthday celebrates all those days when you don't have a birthday at all! And an unbirthday present is given on days when it is not your birthday."

"I see," Alice said, still trying to wipe pie off of her face.

On the bright side, it wasn't on her uniform. It also didn't seem to be making her grow or shrink. "What sort of pie is this?" she repeated.

"Oh a very fine pie," the Hatter assured her. "One fit for a king! It is a middle wish pie."

"What's a—"

"Oh, now that you seem to have stolen the White King's pie, I suppose you'll have to go and apologize to him yourself for being so rude about it," the Mad Hatter said pityingly. "It would really be for the best. I can't go, you see. I am only the messenger that goes and my task is to go elsewhere other than the White King. That is for the March Hare to do, you see, and I can't very well go against my task, now can I?"

"No," Alice said. All things considered, this was probably the best she could ever hope for from a tea party in Wonderland. At least she got to eat something that hadn't gone bad.

"Be sure to tell him it was a middle wish pie when you do," the Mad Hatter said. "It is always good to tell a king very specifically what it is you are apologizing for or else they may not listen. And if an apology isn't listened to then it isn't much of an apology at all, is it?"

"What is a middle wish pie?" she asked.

"Why it grants your middle most desired wish," the Hatter said as if it were the most obvious thing in the world. "There are many types of wishes, you know."

"Are there?" Alice asked. She knew that there was more madness to come out of this and she was ready for it. She could try to puzzle her way through it while she walked to the White King, wherever he was. She continued to try and wipe the pie from her face, now taking small bites of the chunks she pulled off. If it wasn't going to change her body, it might not be so bad. If it really granted wishes, it might be a good thing.

"Oh yes," the Hatter said. "Funny thing is that many wishes are wishes that we don't know we make at all. Sometimes we wish for good things. Those are the most common ones of them all, and really they are quite dull and boring. Everyone has those. They wish for things like pie and more wishes and to rule over everything and making those pies is far too hard and complicated and they taste awful if I do say so myself.

"There's the other wishes that we don't know we're making to ourselves, mostly because we know how silly they are and we don't want to give them any of our time because they are really quite rude. They're wishes that sound quite nice, but really are quite mean and terrible things. They are wishes so that we get sick or break our legs or something else of the like. Maybe that something bad happens somewhere else. They are silly and horrible wishes, really, and they are all just made so that we can get out of things that we would really rather not do. They're nasty things. I try not to have them too often and you should definitely refrain from them. They are very unbecoming wishes. They are also wishes that we make but don't really actually want to come true. When they do, almost everyone ends up regretting them.

"Your middle most wish is the wish that you don't even know you have," the Hatter said, wistful as Alice finished wiping off the pie from her face. "It's that one wish that you have that you don't mind whether or not it ever happens. For me, mine is that all the butter I have on this table is the very best butter. I already know it is the very best butter, so I need not worry for the wish is already so. I simply worry some of the time."

"What brings you here?" the Dormouse asked at last.

"Pardon?" Alice asked, even the Hatter looking down at the Dormouse, more surprised that he was awake without having been awoken than anything else.

"What brings you here?" the Dormouse asked again. "You smell of cat."

The Hatter looked at her oddly, his eyes moving slowly over to her and clearly waiting for her to give him an answer. Alice became suddenly nervous under their gaze, uncertain as she used a napkin to wipe off her face though there was no pie left on it.

"I was pushed into a mirror," Alice said. "The Cheshire Cat showed up at my school, but he looked like a boy when I saw him and he said that Wonderland had changed. I think he thought I should come back and see it for myself, but I don't know why. He called it my half birthday present."

The Mad Hatter looked contemplative for a moment. "So that's where that cat went," the Hatter said. "He said he'd found a way out. I suppose that means he sent you in his place. Or, perhaps, he sent you because you know how to get back out. That cat never did like to share his secrets."

"But I don't know how to get back," Alice said. "Adrianna will probably worry if she wakes up and I'm not there."

"Then perhaps that should have been your middle wish," the Hatter said, shaking his head. "Your middle wish will be granted now that you've eaten the White King's pie. But, alas, it looks like it wasn't. I suppose this means that the cat did send you to replace him in the White King's forces."

"Replace him?" Alice asked. "What did the White King want with a cat in his forces in the first place? What would I even do?"

"Well," the Hatter said, "the first thing you should do is go to find the White King! You will need to apologize for eating his unbirthday pie and tell him of the March Hare and how he is supposed to deliver it, but he seems to have fallen asleep somewhere. The useless thing, never knows what to do."

"Fine," Alice said, getting up. "I'll go to see the White

King. Do you happen to know how to find him? And he better not want to play a game of croquet. I have had enough games with royalty from last time."

"You don't like games any more, Alice?" the Hatter asked, sounding quite amused. "Wonderland has been taken over by cards playing chess. You would do well to learn to love games again if you want to survive to meet the White King at all."

CHAPTER 6

Humpty Dumpty

THE HATTER POINTED her towards the thinner part of the woods to find the White King. She almost expected the Cheshire Cat to drop down from one of the trees to try to tell her something without ever actually saying anything at all.

There was something else that was out of place here that was bothering her. The Mad Hatter and the Dormouse were significantly less maddening to talk to. She knew she wasn't remembering wrong. She'd been made to relive the events so often that she couldn't forget them anymore. No, they definitely weren't as nonsensical as last time.

Was Wonderland becoming less mad? That scared her.

She didn't let herself think about it for long, seeing something strange up ahead. She could have sworn it was a well-dressed egg wandering down the path towards her, stumbling as he went.

Alice thought this was probably a good opportunity to test her theory. If this egg drove her mad, then she would have nothing to worry about.

He kept wandering back and forth as she drew nearer, looking for a place to sit. Every time he'd get close to a rock that looked about right he would trip and try very hard not to smash his head open.

"Well, don't just stand there you— oh!" he said, then tripping over what appeared to be a tart. He stumbled around until he regained his footing. He glared back down at the tart, but it was gone.

Alice wasn't sure if it was madness returning that made a vindictive pastry try to trip one of its own ingredients or if she was just hoping for too much. Still, this seemed an awful lot like madness to her. Maybe he could point the way to the White King.

"I'm sorry," she said, careful to remember her manners. For a land full of rude people, they were always picky about *her* manners. "Did you need a hand?"

"Not until you tell me your name and business," he said, turning to look directly at her and standing stationary for just a moment. Alice realized that he was quite a large egg. He was dressed in fine silks, which looked completely inappropriate for walking around in a forest.

"My name is Alice and—"

"It's a stupid enough name!" Humpty Dumpty pro-claimed, though she was pretty sure that the loudness was due to him tripping once again. She bent forward to catch him just before he fell. He was heavy, but she kept him from crashing to the ground and helped him back to his feet again.

"Maybe you should take a seat," she said quickly as he started to say something else.

"I beg your pardon?" he demanded, appalled that she would dare interrupt him. He pulled himself away from her arms and stared at her, standing tall and trying to look intimi-dating.

Alice just saw a very large egg that was trying desperately to be scary. "You seem to be having some trouble," she said, speaking slowly and deliberately. "I am sorry if I was mis-taken. I only wanted to help."

"*I* do not need any help from little girls," Humpty Dumpty assured her, tripping on another randomly placed treacle tart as he moved closer to another stone. "I am perfectly capable of seating myself, thank you very much."

He certainly tripped quite a bit for someone who didn't need her help, Alice noted. She said nothing, however, try-ing instead to follow how the treacle tart seemed to appear underfoot just as he took a step a little too close to taking a seat on anything else. He never quite stepped on it, his foot catching on the underside of the foil instead and knocking him off balance.

She was getting distracted. She needed to find the White King and find out if Wonderland was really losing its madness.

"A little help isn't a bad thing," Alice told the egg. "If you fell and cracked open, I'd bet not even all the King's horses and all the Kings men could put you back together again."

"Oh, the White King gave me his personal word that if that happens then all his horses and all his men would be right there to pick me back up," Humpty Dumpty said, sounding awfully haughty about it all. "He is just dealing with quite a bit now. I thought it would be best to come down from the wall and not worry him *so*—"

He tripped again. He barely managed to catch himself, the treacle tart vanishing when he turned back to confront it. He let out a growl of frustration and stomped on the ground, but the treacle was still firmly in hiding.

"Oh, so you know the White King?" Alice asked, trying to sound impressed. She only wanted directions, but a little flattery never hurt in Wonderland. Especially since this egg seemed to be a bit full of himself. If she could make him happy and keep him that way, he might escort her right to the White King himself. Besides, if he actually knew the King, the egg might help her find a way to gently break the news that Alice had eaten his unbirthday gift and that his messenger, the Hare, may have been captured by the Queen of Hearts.

"I dare say I should know the White King!" the egg exclaimed, looking outraged that she might imply that it was otherwise. "I am Humpty Dumpty! I am a close, personal friend of the White King. I dare say he would never do anything without speaking to me first!"

Alice bent down, nodding and never dropping her attention from Humpty Dumpty. She quickly reached out to the ground, sweeping the treacle tart out from under Humpty Dumpty's feet. She rose back up, keeping the tart trapped between her fingers.

Humpty Dumpty managed to actually take his seat on the stone, which really did look a little like a shallow wall, and made himself quite comfortable atop it.

"Oh, I see," she said. "He must trust you greatly. Would you like this tart?"

Humpty Dumpty didn't seem to notice the offer, turning what would have been his nose up at it when he began to speak again. "I am one of the White King's most trusted advisors!" he said, puffing himself up as much as an egg could and trying to look very important. "And I am quite trustworthy, mind. He could not have chosen anyone better than I. He came often to visit me at my wall before I came down, but he's terribly busy now."

"Busy you say?" Alice asked as she looked over the treacle in her hands. It didn't have any mushrooms in it from what she could tell, nor did it smell of mushrooms or the caterpillar. There was no sign on it that requested her to consume it. Those signs were always a very clear indication of the best of ill intentions.

It appeared to just be a regular treacle tart with a mischievous streak.

"Kingly business," Humpty Dumpty told her. "The only kind of business that a King concerns himself with! Though right now it is mostly dealing with this business of the Queen of Hearts and her stealing the Red King's heart and taking away the White Queen. He's quite irritated by that part, you see. And there are all sorts of terrible things that have been happening that he's been quite busy with handling. It's why I left my wall, you see. He worries so and I wished to give him less to worry about."

"How thoughtful of you," Alice said, putting the treacle in her pocket. "Perhaps it would be good to go see the White King and see if we couldn't cheer him up."

"That might be an idea," Humpty Dumpty said, rocking a little on his wall. "Indeed, it might even be a good idea, but that would hardly be a task for one such as I, you see. I am quite busy and I must continue to watch. The White King trusts me with a great deal, you see. Although why he had asked me out here where no one passes to watch, I am unsure, but he is the White King and must know what he's speaking of. If you were to go, however, I would recommend something of a gift. It is the White King's unbirthday today and it would be awfully rude to show up without a gift."

"I think I may have something for him," Alice said, noting that the treacle tart might make for a decent substitute for the pie she had unwittingly eaten. "I don't know the way, though. I've never gone to visit the White King before and don't know where to find him."

"Well, I think your manners are a bit more suspect than your sense of direction," Humpty Dumpty said. "One would do well to greet the White King with good manners instead of a good sense of direction."

"But how will I greet the White King at all if I cannot find him?" Alice asked, forcing herself not to say anything about how poor his manners were. It was no use. Besides, this egg was about to give her an actual answer.

"I suppose that is a point to consider," Humpty Dumpty conceded.

Alice could hardly believe she was about to get an answer out of someone in Wonderland. Twice in one day. Something horrible must have happened to Wonderland to make it only rude and insulting instead of outright maddening.

"You there!" she heard amidst a galloping sound approaching from behind her. Alice wanted to curse. She'd been so close, but Humpty Dumpty's attention was on whatever was coming.

She turned to see a great red knight on a great red steed come galloping up. He was twice as big as Alice and coming down the path at full speed, lance in hand and sword fastened to his side.

"Oh dear, not *him*," Humpty Dumpty said, moving very carefully not to trip and fall from atop his wall and instead wriggle his way off. "These horrible knights of the Queen of Hearts' army are so very rude and will not listen to reason or to manners. We will need to leave hastily, but not too quick!"

Alice turned back to help Humpty Dumpty off of his wall. Though she wanted to, this was not the time to point out the irony of him saying that.

"Rotten thing hasn't been duelling by the rules," Humpty Dumpty said. "No proper manners on that one any longer. He's a savage, nothing that any good sort of person should consort with. I should know that rightly, I am close with the White King and he would know better than anyone."

"If we go quickly, we might be able to tell the White King," Alice suggested. She was so close. "He should know that there is someone who is disobeying the rules."

"You there! Halt!" The Red Knight called again, this time sounding much closer.

Alice turned to see how much time they had only to find that he had the end of his lance pointed directly at her. It startled her and she stumbled back.

"You are my prisoner," he informed her, his voice cold and threatening.

Alice looked back to Humpty Dumpty, who was more concerned with hiding than heading to the White King. So close. She had been so close to actually have someone in Wonderland help her. The madness was fading enough that she might have had an actual answer from someone. And now that she'd come so close, someone was actually threatening her?

"No!" she said, turning back to the knight and pushing the lance away from her. "I don't know if you realize this, since very few people in Wonderland know how manners actually work despite how often they feel they need to correct mine, but it's not very polite to interrupt a conversation or point things at a person."

The knight didn't waver on his horse. "You are my prisoner," the Red Knight repeated, raising his lance again.

"I said no!" Alice said, once more pushing the lance out of the way, her heart beating furiously in her chest. This was weird. He was supposed to tell her she was rude or tell her she was wrong. She was starting to think he might actually hurt her.

Still, this was Wonderland.

"In order to be a prisoner, I'd have to be a damsel in distress," she reasoned. "That's the sort of prisoner you knights typically take. Damsels in distress. Well, as you can see, I am just a girl who is a little lost for the moment. Hardly a damsel and not at all in distress. That makes me quite the bad prisoner. I would suggest you find another girl that is more befitting of being a prisoner."

"I do not play your games, girl," the Red Knight informed her.

Alice was taken aback. No one had ever spoken so directly to her here. It was like he wasn't even from Wonderland at all. She didn't know what she was going to do about it or how to talk her way out of it. Her words died as the fear overtook her.

"You are my prisoner. That is all there will be to it. Come along."

"I think not!" Alice said, though she was terrified. This was wrong. Wonderland didn't do any of this. She had to say something or do something before anyone threatened her, and no one had ever tried to kidnap her before. It was like the madness had faded away completely in the Red Knight.

For a moment, she thought it worked. The knight raised his lance and permitted Alice to pass. She glanced back at Humpty Dumpty, who continued to cower behind her, and shook her head. She'd find someone else to help her, but for now she needed to get away from the Red Knight.

She turned back to go, but the Red Knight nudged the horse closer to her and reached down. He snatched Alice up by the arm and brought her up to look at her. She struggled against his pull, trying to wriggle out of his grasp.

"I told you no!" she said. "Let me go! Put me down! This is very rude!" She knew she sounded like a scared twelve year old girl, but she tried to remain brave and struggle out of his grasp.

The Red Knight laid her down over the front of his horse, the tart squishing in her pocket, and looked down to Humpty Dumpty as he finally stopped cowering. Instead he stood up tall, looking indignant that the Red Knight had dared to take away the person he was hiding behind.

"Now, that is going quite too far!" Humpty Dumpty said, stamping a foot on the ground. "Unhand her at once. She may be rude, but you have exhibited even more rudeness and blatant violation of the rules that cannot be permissible. Unhand her and obey the proper rules."

The Red Knight did not move and continued to stare down at him. Humpty Dumpty visibly shrank under his gaze. She wanted to tell him not to do anything rash, but she didn't get the chance. Humpty Dumpty's knees wavered and he stepped back as if he were going to turn to run. As he did so, he stepped on a rock and tripped, falling and this time crashing into the wall upon which he was previously perched.

The bits and pieces of Humpty Dumpty dropped all at once as he shattered into many pieces. He had a great fall and it seemed that he was in so many pieces that he would never be put back together again.

The Red Knight brought his horse around and started to ride off.

"Wait!" Alice said, shocked. "We have to help him! He's been shattered!"

The Red Knight looked at her for only a moment. Alice knew behind the cold helmet was just as cold a face looking at her and silently demanding to know why he should do anything about it. It was as he had said, apparently. She was his prisoner and that was all there was to it.

They started to ride off, Alice considering trying to jump from the horse, but not seeing how she would get away. The knight in his armour clattered against a sword and several smaller knives that she could see now that she was on the horse with him.

Wonderland had changed. It had changed more than she could imagine.

"Pardon me," she said, trying to keep the fear out of her voice and her eyes off his weapons. "Please, why have I been taken prisoner?"

"The Queen has demanded all the hearts in the kingdom be brought to her," he said. "You have yet to give her your heart and that makes you a criminal. We will keep you in the castle until you comply with the rules of the kingdom."

"But I didn't know the rule!" Alice said.

"Ignorance is hardly an excuse," the Red Knight said and Alice fell quiet. She was trapped and she didn't know what she was going to do or say to get herself out of this mess. She was terrified, but there was nothing she could think to do. She hoped for a white knight to save her, but no one came. And so Alice became the prisoner of the Red Knight.

CHAPTER 7

Jail Bird King

ALICE VERY QUICKLY learned that Wonderland prison really was nothing special. On her way in, she saw that the castle, while being wondrous and huge, was still just a castle, complete with moat and a drawbridge that lowered at the Red Knight's command. Inside, nothing sang or asked tricky puzzles or did much of anything out of the ordinary. And now she was down in a very ordinary sort of prison in a very ordinary sort of cell and locked with a very ordinary sort of lock. The only thing even slightly abnormal about any of this was that the jailer was a bird wearing red.

When nothing moved and nothing spoke and nothing wanted to tell her how rude she was, Alice realized that Wonderland was suffering from sanity instead of madness, and the sanity was spreading. None of Wonderland seemed to be the way it once was. Alice didn't know what caused this, but she was certain that she should probably do something. While she still had her heart, anyway.

The Red Knight had puzzled her with that one. It was mentioned a few times already that the Queen had gone quite mad herself and demanded people's hearts instead of their heads, but Alice couldn't understand what that *meant*. How do you steal a heart? Aside from the obvious pun of falling in love, she had no idea.

Alice was so tired. Cat had woken her in the middle of the night and it was starting to catch up with her. She sat back against the cold stone wall and closed her eyes, letting herself drift off while trying to think of something that could get her out of this cell.

When she opened her eyes again, she wasn't alone. Sitting in the next cell was man dressed in white. He rose to his feet, about as tall as Evan when he was upright, and he looked down at her kindly. He had no crown, but even Alice understood the regal bearing to him.

"So they've brought me a visitor," he said, the man sounding quite humourless.

Alice scrambled to her feet and dipped into a deep bow as a show of respect, but the White King waved his hand to stop her. He looked tired, no smile in his eyes, only a deep sense of fatigue. He seemed like he might have once been the usual person of Wonderland, fully ready to correct her manners, but perhaps a little time here had done something to him. Or maybe he'd had his heart stolen too.

"There's no need to bow," he said. "I am hardly a King anymore. I've been in here long enough that I know that."

"You still have many loyal followers," Alice said. "The Mad Hatter and Humpty Dumpty have both said so."

He said nothing, seeming to consider this for a very long while. He moved, pacing back and forth in a very small corner of his cell, though it seemed he could have moved a great deal more if he wanted to. He looked out the bars of the cell to the bird and then back to Alice. "What are you here for?" he asked finally. "What business do you have with the Queen of Hearts?"

"None that I know of," Alice said. "I had business with her once, I guess. I attempted to play croquet properly with her the last time I came to Wonderland and she demanded that my head come off. It was... unpleasant."

"I would imagine so," the White King said, mostly humourless, though Alice thought she saw a bit of a glimmer in his eyes. "And the Queen has not yet stolen your own heart, I take it?"

Alice shook her head. "Not yet, though I hope she doesn't take it at all. I like my heart right where it is. From what I've heard, the Queen has stolen quite a few hearts but, I beg your pardon, I don't understand what that means."

"Begging isn't becoming," the White King said. "Situation being as it is or not, one should always try not to beg if it can be helped. But if I'm not mistaken, you are not of Wonderland properly. It would do you well to remember to state your name firstly when addressing royalty."

"My name is Alice," Alice said, looking a little embarrassed and sinking herself into a curtsy. This time, the White King leaned his head in to greet her back. "But I still don't understand what she means by stealing hearts or how you knew I wasn't from Wonderland. When I was here last, everyone seemed to expect that I was and thought I was rude for not knowing the rules or their manners."

"Oh, it really is quite obvious," the White King said. "I suspect the last time you were here, they merely thought it would be a bit of fun to tease you as we often do with one another. Though some are just mad enough to miss the obvious. Had circumstances been different, I imagine I would have been correcting you as well, but I see no need to do that in our current predicament."

Alice really didn't have anything to offer to that, though she was getting a bit thirsty. Bowing a little to excuse herself, she went back to the bars of their cell and leaned out, looking to the bird on the other side of the hall.

"Pardon me!" she called. "Pardon me, but could I please have a drink of water?"

The bird looked back at her, his eyes soulless, then slowly looked away. He was quite a lovely bird other than those eyes, Alice had to admit. He had a lovely brown plumage and was quite large for a bird. He wore a bright red tunic, probably marking him as a part of the Red King's army.

"Don't bother," the White King said, Alice stepping away from the bars. "The jail bird has never been quite the same since the Queen of Hearts took his heart away. He's been quite quiet and only moves when someone leaves. So long as you are here, he will not do a thing, much less fetch you water."

"Are you sure you still have your heart?" Alice asked suddenly, a little bothered that he was making quite so much sense. "You are speaking a bit too plainly to be a King in Wonderland, if you'll pardon my saying so."

The King sighed heavily. "I do suppose that is true," the White King said. "I have learned a great deal sitting in here. Wonderland is no longer the place it once was and there is a great something missing. I have had to adjust to this new way, though I am not at all happy about it. I am, however, a King. When I reclaim Wonderland, then all will fall back into place."

"I hope not everything," Alice said. "I liked not having everyone around me tell me that I'm rude and have poor manners this time. I think Wonderland could get used to a change like this if it needed to."

The White King let out a small laugh at that. His laugh sounded old, like he hadn't used it in quite a while and it had gotten a little rusty.

"Ah, Alice," he said with his small smile. "I should hope that you return to Wonderland often and become the jester in my court. Humour comes with a dose of truth and it seems that you have the bravery to speak the truth to even a king, even if that king is quite stuck in a cell."

"Don't you have knights?" Alice asked. "They could come to rescue you."

"I'm afraid my Knights are somewhat preoccupied," the White King said. "One is already fallen and another has vowed to rescue damsels in distress. I doubt he's fared very well. He's always had a rather terrible sense of humour and was quite clumsy. I wonder if he's still even out there. I know my second Knight is in here, staying but a few doors over and still lamenting the loss of his battle with the Red Knight."

"Oh!" Alice said, remembering why she wanted to find the White King in the first place. "Your Majesty, I came to see you with an apology. I'm afraid there was an accident when I went to see the Mad Hatter. The March Hare had forgotten the Unbirthday present he meant to bring you and it unwittingly landed instead on me."

The White King looked at her like she had just told him that the grass was usually green. "That hardly matters, dear," he said. "I have hardly had time to worry about unbirthdays since I've been in here. There have been somewhat more pressing matters to attend to."

Alice sat on the ground at the bars to watch the Jail Bird, who didn't look like himself. She'd never met him before, but she was sure that no large bird in Wonderland should look or act quite like that. He seemed to be a little more like the birds back home instead of anything from Wonderland except that his chest, instead of puffing out proudly, looked like it had fallen in a little.

And then she thought of something.

"Pardon me, Mr. Jail Bird?" she called, going back to stick her head out the bars again. When the Jail Bird turned its slow head around to face her, she took the treacle tart out of her pocket, somewhat surprised that it was still intact. "Would you care for a piece of treacle tart?"

The Jail Bird seemed to perk up a little at that and hop over to see the tart a little better. Alice waved it outside of the cell for only a moment before bringing it very quickly back in and out of the Jail Bird's reach.

The White King was offended. "If you had something,

you would do well to remember your manners," the White King said. "You have already ruined my unbirthday present and now you have a treacle tart and do not offer it first to the king?"

Alice continued to lure the Jail Bird closer to her cell door. "You're very right, Your Majesty," she said, keeping her eyes on the Jail Bird. "I simply thought our jailer might be hungry. He does have to watch us all day, after all. And if he's quite that hungry, then perhaps he could open the door and join us in here and we can all share the treacle tart."

The Jail Bird made a grab for the tart, Alice not quick enough to pull her hand away. His beak nipped at her hand, but the tart wasn't there. The Jail bird looked at her longingly and then moved back to his perch.

Alice snapped her hand back into the cell, rubbing at her palm and inspecting the damage. It was just a small mark that didn't appear to be bleeding, but it still stung. Once she was satisfied that it was a small injury, she looked around to see where she dropped the tart.

The King didn't even seem to notice that the tart had vanished at all. He looked annoyed that the plan didn't work.

Alice found the treacle on the ground where she had taken a nap. There didn't appear to be any dirt on it. Come to think of it, she'd squashed it when she was taken prisoner, but it looked perfectly fine.

"Does treacle tart make you shrink or grow?" Alice asked, her stomach starting to rumble. It would be about breakfast now, she figured.

"Don't be absurd," the White King said. "Why ever would a treacle tart make you change size?"

"Would you like some?" Alice asked, watching his reaction carefully.

"No thank you, dear," he said, settling right back into the corner. He seemed to have gotten his hopes up a little too high and sunk right back to being down once again, depressed and, Alice presumed, lamenting for his lost madness. His heart, he claimed, was still there but he seemed to be losing his madness like the rest of Wonderland. She wasn't sure what was going on.

He also didn't seem to be refusing the treacle for any reasons relating to what it might do to him. She shrugged and decided it might be safe. She took a nibble of it first, waiting anxiously for a moment to find out if it was going to make her grow or shrink. Come to think of it, either of those would actually be rather useful right about now. If she were larger, she might be able to simply remove the bars to let them out. If she were smaller, then she could slip through the bars. This time, however, the treacle tart was just a treacle tart.

It was a nice tart, lovely and very sweet. It was smooth and she rather wished there was something else to have with it. The more she ate of it, the more it felt like it was too sweet for her. Hunger alone made her finish it, leaving her hungry still and even more thirsty.

Alice looked to the White King. "If the Jail Bird doesn't bring water, how do you manage when you get thirsty?"

"Oh, I usually imagine myself a glass of water," the King said dismissively. "Something nice and tall and cool. You don't quite get that down here, even if you are a king. They don't know how to treat guests and their manners are appalling."

Alice blinked, but held her tongue. Had he really been surviving on imaginary water? There had to be a trick at work here. Maybe when he closed his eyes to imagine it, something put a glass of water in his hands.

He was staring at her, so she decided to try imagining herself a glass of water in somewhere a bit nicer than this. Her mind wandered and she pictured the tall glass of water first, cool and with just a bit of condensation on the side. She imagined she was in the dining room of the Queen. She could hear the Queen of Hearts yelling at her cards and almost see those cards, all of them blank instead of bearing their respective numbers of hearts. There was even the Jack of Hearts, looking quite blank himself and not sure what to make of the Red King in the room, who sat emotionless and looking lost.

She reached out a hand and took a glass of water off of the table, all of it set with a great amount of finery and several places set out, though no one looked as if they were allowed to sit at any of them. One of the blank cards looked over. Alice nodded and smiled to the card and closed her eyes, not sure why her imagination was quite so vivid today. It was nice, but really all she wanted was that glass of water.

When she opened her eyes again, she was still in her cell, but this time with a glass of water in her hand. She was about to drink, then pulled the glass away and looked it over carefully to check it. Not a mushroom, nor were there any mushrooms or pastries in it. Nothing told her to drink it. And the treacle tart had been safe. She was probably worried over nothing, but she eyed the glass of water, looking for anything odd about it.

"Did you say that was a treacle tart?" the White King asked from his cell, rising back to his feet and staring down at her.

"It was, Your Majesty," she said, looking from the glass of water to him. She wondered if she could make him drink some of it first to see if it did anything. It was only polite to share with a king, after all.

The White King nodded to himself. "Humpty Dumpty has come down off of his wall, then?"

"Yes, Your Majesty," Alice said, confused again. "If you'll

pardon me, what does Humpty Dumpty have to do with treacle tarts?"

"You see," he said carefully, "there was a time when whatever a King or Queen said would become law. Humpty Dumpty fancied himself a very valued confidant of mine and implied that he was far more valuable than the White Queen, my dear wife, one day while she was present. As you can imagine, saying such a thing is quite an insult to a Queen. It was on that day that she sentenced him to sit on the wall and watch for anything coming, but never to come down again or he would slip on a treacle tart and crack himself into a thousand pieces."

"Why a treacle tart?" Alice asked, though she wished she could take it back. This happened back when the madness of Wonderland was in full force. She was going to regret this.

"My wife quite likes treacle tarts," the White King said almost dismissively. "Humpty Dumpty didn't believe such a thing and went back to sit atop his wall. When he came down next, he started noticing that there was a treacle tart following him about. Whenever he would draw near something that it would be quite unwise to fall into, there was the treacle tart underfoot, trying to make him trip and fall."

The king pondered it for a moment, seeming to have frozen himself in a moment of contemplation before continuing. "He only ever attended one more meeting after that. He said that the Cheshire Cat ate the treacle tart that got in his way on his way there and all my horses and all my men worked together to put him back atop his wall before my wife smashed him in herself. Apparently she found a way to replace the tart to keep him away."

"I suppose that makes sense," Alice said, knowing it didn't make any sense at all.

"Have you ever pondered how the Cheshire Cat manages to appear and disappear as he wishes?" the White King asked, a small grin growing on his lips, bitter more than anything else.

"Well," Alice pondered, letting the word carry for a while. "I suppose it's just how he is."

"And what would make him that way?" the King asked.

If he weren't a King, Alice might have tried ignoring the question. Unfortunately, he seemed to be having fun trying to make her guess what had happened. She fully expected him to tell her she was stupid for not understanding what he was talking about.

And then she got it. "You are what you eat," she said. "So if he ate a treacle that was meant to disappear and reappear underfoot, then he's now a cat that disappears and reappears underfoot."

"Quite," the King told her. "Though it seems that he's chosen whose foot to get under now. And now that you have eaten the same treacle as the cat, it seems that you will now be getting underfoot and leaving me here while you go off to irritate others much as the Cheshire Cat has chosen to."

"Are you saying I disappeared to get a glass of water, and then appeared back here?"

The King nodded.

"Of course," Alice said, unimpressed. Of course eating something in Wonderland would change her. Hopefully she would find something to counteract it before she left. Or maybe it would fade away on its own once she left. Or maybe drinking the glass of water would cancel out the effects.

Not that she wanted to yet. If she could get out of her cell, she might be able to free the White King and do whatever it was she was meant to do before the Cheshire Cat could pull her out. Or Wonderland would kick her out when she was done. She still had no idea what she was supposed to do here.

She paced around her cell, glass of water in hand. One problem at a time. She was worried that she was going to start suddenly appearing and disappearing without any warning or reason soon. She needed to come up with a logical reason to not go vanishing randomly into anywhere that her imagination took her. She needed to outsmart the pastry.

"The treacle has a reason to appear under Humpty Dumpty's foot," she said. "That reason for the treacle was given to it by the White Queen. It was ordered to appear underfoot, but it wouldn't do that if it wasn't ordered to. And the Cheshire Cat, he's a cat. Cats like to get themselves underfoot at the least opportune moments, not all the time. So being irritating and appearing underfoot is not a part of it, only disappearing and reappearing, right?"

"Perhaps," the King said. "I suppose your logic is sound. I am not quite in my own right mind right now, however, so I have quite the difficulty knowing one way or another. The rules of Wonderland don't make the same sort of sense they used to. It's a different sort of sense that has me quite baffled."

Alice took that as Wonderland accepting her logic. "What will this glass of water do?" she asked.

"It will be a glass of water."

"What will happen to me if I drink it?"

"I suppose you will not be thirsty anymore."

"Will anything other than that happen to me?"

"Of course not," the White King said. "It is only water."

She took a sip of it and continued to consider her new predicament. She had eaten the treacle and she had accidentally disappeared, appeared in the Queen's dining room and then vanished again back into her cell. Could she do that with anywhere in the castle? Or could she leave the castle into anywhere in Wonderland? Maybe she could just go home.

"It is quite rude to take things without asking," the

King said, looking at the glass. "I would suggest that you return that."

"And what would I do once that is done?" she asked. She still didn't know what she was supposed to do here in order to go back home. Was there a goal this time, or was it like before, where she was here until she wasn't anymore? "Should I come back and rescue his majesty? It would be awfully rude to break out of jail without the king."

"If nothing is broken, then it is hardly breaking out of jail," the White King pointed out. "You are merely leaving and may go without requesting my blessing. I would request, however, if you see my free white knight that you request he come to release myself and his brother from these cells. This is hardly befitting of a king."

"Thank you, Your Majesty," Alice said. "Do you know where I might escape to? Perhaps somewhere that I could be of some help."

"I'd suggest trying to find the Queen of Heart's room of hearts," the White King suggested. "It is there she keeps all the hearts of Wonderland. If you could, it would be most beneficial of you to return some of the hearts to the people of Wonderland so that this land may start to make some proper sense again."

That sounded like a goal. It was something of a direction to go now that she wasn't following a path, anyway. "I will do what I can, Your Majesty," she said, bowing deeply in her curtsy to the White King and thinking of the dining room where she had stolen the glass of water.

CHAPTER 8

The Red Knight and the White Knight

THEN SHE WAS back in the dining room where she was only moments ago. The Queen of Hearts was now yelling more viciously at one particular card. Her voice was as shrill as Alice remembered it and, this time, Alice listened to her as she set the glass back down. She even poured water back into it so that it would look like she never took a drink at all.

"A girl! There was no girl there!" the Queen of Hearts yelled at the blank card, who didn't seem all that concerned he was being yelled at. He looked back over to Alice and Alice knew it was time to take her leave.

"Your Majesty," the card said, pointing once again to Alice. Alice curtsied deep and wished she was back in the jail cell with the King as the card said, "She's returned again."

Alice closed her eyes, thinking about how nice the other side of the wall might be. A nice red wall with a faint heart print on it.

When she opened her eyes again, she was in the hall. She took no time to admire her ability and followed the hall, not sure where she should go next. Out here she could smell something cooking, likely the kitchen getting ready for whatever feast the table had been set for. Perhaps she should look for the kitchen and get something to eat before she continued looking for the room of hearts.

Alice followed the smell. She made her way down to the kitchen, finding it to be full and bustling with diamond cards that worked tirelessly to get the food prepared. There were a few other creatures scattered about at work as well, but Alice hardly paid attention to any of it. There was a lot of stuff happening in here, pies being baked and turkeys coming out of the oven and, besides the things that were actually doing the cooking, everything seemed perfectly normal.

More and more, the normalcy of Wonderland was starting to completely and utterly disturb her. It was Wonderland, a place of magical wonderment and nonsense. Here in the kitchen, though, they didn't even notice she was there at all, too engrossed in their work to reprimand her for rudely intruding.

Her eyes were drawn to a small forest in the corner of the kitchen that no one else was giving a second thought to. There were pots, pans and cutlery hanging in the branches to dry and threatening to fall on anyone who stayed too long under them.

Peeling carrots beneath a tree of pots was a very familiar hare. Her heart jumped and she made her way through the kitchen, careful not to be in anyone's way. They were too absorbed in their task, like they were stuck in a trance and didn't even look up when she brushed past them.

She knelt down next to the March Hare, though he didn't look at her. He was busy working through a pail of carrots. His eyes looked dull, his mind elsewhere. She reached out a tentative hand to touch him on the arm, but he didn't react to it.

"Hello?" she asked, her eyes darting back to the kitchen and she kept her voice low. "March Hare? I'm Alice. We had tea once."

He stopped, his head turning slowly to look at her. "Is that so?" he asked, sounding tired, each of his words very slow and deliberate.

"Yes," she said. "The Mad Hatter has been worried. You were supposed to come back."

"I see," he said. He turned back to the carrots.

"You should go back!"

"No. I must do as my Queen asks. You would do best to do the same."

Alice rose and backed away until she bumped into one of the trees, the pots above her banging together but they did not fall. It looked like the March Hare, but it wasn't him. He had none of the energy or the madness. He didn't scold her for interrupting him or not working. He seemed so normal, except for being a large talking hare.

She looked around at the people in the kitchen. They all looked just as soulless as the March Hare had. Had the Queen of Hearts done this?

Why had she even come down here? She was still hungry, but her stomach was starting to tie itself into knots. Everything was so normal. For Wonderland, it was completely wrong. Where was the madness? There had to be something unusual happening.

She started to make her way back through the kitchen again. She had to get out of here and find something strange and out of place. Anything that might tell her that Wonderland was still the land of madness she remembered.

When she heard the clomping of horse hooves in the kitchen she was almost relieved. A horse inside the castle was out of place. Maybe not quite as out of place as she would like, certainly not at the point of madness, but it was something.

Really, not enough strange things were happening for her liking right now.

Alice turned slowly around to find the Red Knight there,

though without his horse. He stood there, looking down at her with cold eyes and his helmet off. His eyes reminded her of the March Hare's, completely emotionless and dull. He carried his helmet in one hand and his other hand rested on his sword.

The galloping was still there and approaching, though she could not tell where from.

"You were my prisoner from earlier," the Red Knight said.

"I may have been," she said carefully, stepping back. "But clearly I am not anymore. There is no need to concern yourself with the likes of me. You're probably quite busy taking several prisoners for the Queen of Hearts."

"I don't play these games any longer," the Red Knight said, the galloping hooves still echoing and drawing ever closer. Alice backed away as the Red Knight stepped forward menacingly. "You are my prisoner."

"I think not!" another voice said. There, the source of the galloping burst into the kitchen and someone came up on a white horse. Atop the saddle was a knight all dressed in white, presumably the White Knight that was going after damsels in distress. Well, right about now she would count herself as someone in quite a lot of distress.

The Red Knight's reaction was slow, turning to look right as the White Knight rushed past on his horse and struck him hard on the side of his armour with his lance. The Red Knight reeled and fell backwards, the White Knight looping back and bowing to Alice once his horse came to a stop before her. Alice looked warily at the Red Knight, who seemed to be down but nowhere near out.

"My lady, are you quite all right?" the White Knight asked her, Alice looking back up at him. When he lifted the visor of his helmet, there was the face of a British man with a bushy moustache looking down at her with a great deal of concern. "I am quite sorry about my conduct, but you must understand. The Red Knight was once a fine opponent, but he has since denied following the proper rules of battle. As such, I have been forced to follow in suit lest something terrible happen to me as it has to my king and my comrades."

"Thank you," Alice said, her eyes flickering back to the Red Knight, who was now putting on his helmet. "I don't think he is going to observe the rule that says that he's supposed to stay down, though. If there is really a rule."

"Oh my," the White Knight said. "Well, I would suggest you hide somewhere while I deal with this ruffian," the White Knight said, dismounting. "I say, we should be on even ground this time. While you have decided not to observe the rules of combat, I am still not one to take an opponent fully at a disadvantage at all times."

Alice thought that was a terrible idea, but she wasn't going to argue the point. She dashed through the kitchen, trying to find a place to hide. She found herself underneath a small table where there were a few cats peeling potatoes, saying nothing and not even noticing her there.

No one seemed to mind that there were two fully armed knights that waged battle in their kitchen either, swords flailing wildly as the two met each other blow for blow. The Red Knight was considerably more practiced and had the advantage on the White Knight. Still, the White Knight continued to fight hard and Alice wished there was something she could do to help.

She looked around for something that she might be able to throw at the Red Knight, hoping that might throw him off and give the White Knight a better chance. All she could find under the table was a very small cake sitting there with the words "Eat me" on it.

"Oh, I remember you," she said, her eyes glaring down at the small cake. She leaned out from under the table and looked up on top of it. There, sitting just in front of the potatoes was a small basket of mushrooms with another little sign on them. "From the Caterpillar." She looked between the two of them and shook her head. Wonderland was doing this to her on purpose.

Still, if she were bigger, then she might be able to throw something bigger from farther away. As much as she wanted to take down the Red Knight so he wouldn't come after her again, she didn't want to get in the middle of the swords.

She looked around and saw nothing suitable for throwing. If Wonderland was going to taunt her with the cake and mushrooms again, it needed to give her a little more to work with.

Her eyes caught the trees by the March Hare. She could work with those.

She left the safety of hiding under the table with the cake in one hand, her other taking a couple of the mushrooms and putting them in her pocket. She hoped that they were from the same caterpillar and they were from the shrinking side of the mushroom.

She looked over to see the White Knight get knocked down and narrowly miss a blow from the Red Knight, rolling away and trying to get quickly to his feet. There wasn't much time if she were going to help.

Alice ate the cake as soon as she was close to the forest. Her head hit the ceiling and she expanded enough to push the March Hare out of the way. "I'm sorry," she said.

The March Hare did not react.

She looked at the trees and she saw that they weren't resting their pots and pans in the trees, but actually growing them. There were pots, pans and ovens amidst other things. And inwards a little, there was one that sprouted a different sort of fruit in different colours, this one in the variety of fridges.

"Why are—" she began, but she didn't want to know why there were fridges in Wonderland. She had asked for madness and Wonderland had responded with giving her cakes and fridge trees.

She reached over to the fridge tree and picked an avocado green one out. She threw it over to the other side of the room. It was quite a bit lighter than she thought it might be and went right over both of their heads. It smashed against the other wall harmlessly.

Alice wasn't sure if it was because she was larger and much stronger. It was a tree in Wonderland that seemed to be behaving like a tree in Wonderland, though. In those terms, she thought it was light because it was green and green fruit was generally not yet ready to be picked.

She picked another one, this time a golden yellow one that had a little more weight to it. She took aim and tossed it again, this time only just missing the Red Knight as it flew between the two of them. The White Knight turned to look at the very large Alice standing in the corner next to the trees, as did the Red Knight.

She picked the last fridge in the garden, one that was this time powder blue, and threw it directly at the Red Knight. He didn't move out of the way, still staring at Alice. It hit him, knocking him down and pinning him to the ground.

Alice quickly reached into her pocket and pulled out the mushrooms, nibbling a little bit of one. She shrank immediately and Alice checked herself over to make sure that she wasn't long of neck or disproportionate in any way.

When she decided she wasn't, she rushed over to the White Knight and looked him over to see if he was hurt. "I suggest we run before the Red Knight decides to awaken again," she said, pulling him along with her and out of the kitchen.

The White Knight barely registered what was happening as he followed.

They made it out of the kitchen and snaked down several halls before Alice finally stopped, needing to catch her breath.

"My dear," the White Knight said, "I don't think that was quite proper of you. I should have been the one to save you. It's my job, you see."

Alice looked up at him, not in the mood for his disbelief. "You looked like you needed a hand."

"Oh, indeed I did!" the White Knight admitted. "I just should not have accepted it. Myself and the Red Knight, we were in a duel and I should have been able to accept my defeat graciously."

"I didn't want to be taken prisoner again," Alice informed

him. "If you were defeated, he would have come right back after me. I thought helping you would have been a good thing."

"But it was hardly proper. The Red Knight hadn't attacked you yet, nor was it your turn. I was still doing battle with him at the time. It's just not the proper order of things, you see, and you have demonstrated yourself to be quite unladylike."

Alice knew enough to expect this. Of course she would do something nice for someone and they would be ungrateful. At least he was still mad enough to worry that she was being rude, despite the Red Knight attempting to separate his head from his shoulders. She lowered her shoulders as she regained her breath and looked up at him.

"I am sorry," she said. "I only wanted you to be all right. I didn't realize that it would offend you if I came to your aid."

The White Knight seemed to accept it. Alice suspected it was more because she was young and like she was probably going to be in need of even more saving later on. That was fine for now. She might need the backup. There was something odd happening here.

"I suppose I can forgive you then," the White Knight said. "If you are truly sorry."

"Oh, I am," Alice assured him. "I'm very sorry. Though if I may ask, why were you inside the castle on horseback? Where did your horse go?"

"He'll be along shortly," the White Knight said dismissively. "He can always find me again. I am here because I must save the most desperate damsel in distress of all and here is where I must be to rescue her. It is my duty, my calling to rescue her."

"And who is she?" Alice asked, already dreading the answer.

"Why Wonderland, of course," the White Knight said, Alice mentally kicking herself for not seeing that one coming. "She is the greatest damsel in the land and she is in great trouble. Surely you've seen from just here, everything has gone so very wrong and my quest to rescue her has brought me here."

"Really," Alice said. "And what do you need to do to free Wonderland?"

"Why, free the hearts of Wonderland!" he said. "But how to do so is the tricky part. You see, the Queen of Hearts has them all stored in the room of hearts which I have yet to find. But there's much more to it than that, oh so much more!"

"More?" she asked, interested again. She hoped he actually knew something. "What more is there than saving the hearts of Wonderland?"

"There is the matter of how the Queen of Hearts steals the hearts, you see," he said, leaning in close to speak very directly with Alice. "She has discovered a book. It struck the King of Hearts dead and when she read it, she learned of a way to take the hearts of the people so that she could rule all the land always. The book also is said to contain the ability to reverse the Queen of Heart's menacing, but I have yet to find it for I do not know what it looks like."

The White Knight looked around before continuing. "I looked through the entire library, but I am beginning to think that it may be in the room of hearts or someplace that only the Queen of Hearts can get to. I have even looked for the room of hearts, but have yet to find it. The White King knows what the book looks like and where it might be kept, but he has been missing for quite a while and so I have been looking for him as well. He has been a bit harder, as a king is never a damsel and damsels are my specialty."

"The White King is in the prison cells being guarded by the jail bird," Alice said.

"Is he truly here?" the White Knight asked, perking up. "Then I must rescue my King!"

Alice was going to say something when she heard the galloping of hooves. She looked around and the White Knight turned to greet his horse as it came towards him.

"Now that you have your next quest, I will bid you adieu," Alice said, trying to speak more like the knight. Her mind on the White King, she dipped into a deep curtsy.

When Alice rose, she was back in her cell facing the White

King. He rose to meet her. "Hello again," the White King said. "You appear to be quite poor at escaping from prison."

"I need to know something," Alice said. "I met with the White Knight; the one that isn't here. He's in the castle. He will be coming for you soon. In the meantime, he told me of a book that the Queen of Hearts apparently has been using to remove hearts."

"Yes," the White King said. "She keeps the book in the room of hearts."

"What does the book look like?" Alice asked. "If you could please tell me, Your Majesty. If I get the book from her, I may be able to help Wonderland."

"Of course," the White King said. "Anything for the sake of Wonderland. The book is a deep brown and leather with a great and terrible beast inscribed on the front. The words on it are written the wrong way, so I could not read it, but the script was printed in a very fine gold. The edges of the pages were also crested with a golden leaf, though that was wearing down as it seemed quite aged. It was a hefty book and smelled of a forest and ice. The whole book was worn, however, not just the pages, and looked well travelled."

"Thank you," Alice said, dipping once more into a deep curtsy and disappearing from sight.

CHAPTER 9

The Room of Hearts

WHEN ALICE LOOKED up from her curtsy, there was a book in front of her. It was kept on a table with a glass cover over it that she knew she wasn't meant to touch. It was just like the king had described, brown and old with a beast on the cover that she'd never seen before. It looked like something that Wonderland wouldn't have even been able to come up with. The whole thing seemed a little off and, as she rose, she quickly looked around to find out just where she was.

This was definitely the room of hearts. The walls were not only lined, but seemed to actually be made of hearts. Not hearts like the ones that the queen wore. Instead, the walls moved, beating together and, while the glass that held them back and in place was iced over so that she couldn't see them exactly, they looked like they were literal hearts. When she looked down, the floor was the same, only this time tinted in red and looking almost like they were sitting in blood instead of still beating in the ice.

Her brain started to shut down from looking at it, but she didn't have time for that. There was a door on one side of the room made of regular wood, unlike everything else in here, and voices just outside it that she could hear over the soft beating of the hearts.

She needed to hide and she looked madly around for something that wasn't made out of the hearts of Wonderland to cower behind.

There was a small wooden desk in the room that she hid under, though she found out very quickly that she was wrong about it as well. The exterior was only stained to look like wood. Inside, a loose pack of hearts floated freely, shifting and moving, letting her see through the small gaps in them as someone entered followed by several more people. All of them seemed rather familiar.

"I almost don't know where I will put your heart," the woman in the lead said with a bit of a laugh. "I already have so many. Perhaps I'm being a touch greedy. Then again, there is nothing too great for a Queen." She laughed.

Alice felt a chill run down her spine and her breath catch in her throat.

It was the Queen of Hearts, but was very different from when Alice had last seen her. For one, she was no longer the heavy-set queen in loud, heart-themed clothing anymore. Instead, she was slender, taller, and wore a very elegant heart themed dress with a touch of silver to offset all of the red. She was younger too, and had her hair done up delicately atop her head, no longer wearing the large headpiece and opting instead for a much simpler crown that hid nothing of her newfound elegance. Her voice, however, had not changed.

With her was the White Rabbit, looking somewhat dazed at all of the hearts in the room and not saying a word as he looked around. He looked quite worse for wear, like he'd gone several days running through the woods without tea or anything else to eat, and seeming sluggish on his feet. He wasn't in a hurry this time, and instead seemed scared, but too weak to do anything. He stumbled along under the arms of two young men in red armour.

"Come along," the Queen of Hearts said, sounding amused. Indeed, she seemed to have a spring in her step, quite pleased with whatever was about to happen. Alice shifted to the left to see more, a heart drifting into her vision. "Oh, come along you damn Rabbit. It took long enough to find you with all your moving about. We have cleared your appointments indefinitely now, though. You'll never be late for anything again. Doesn't that sound quite lovely?"

The White Rabbit seemed to go even paler, a renewed

sense of resistance swelling up in him. "Oh, I don't *mind* being late, per se," he said quickly. "It's really more that I'm late because I'm forgetful. Always forgetting my gloves and my fan, and my watch runs a touch slow, but these are all things that can be fixed with my heart still intact."

"I don't think so," the Queen of Hearts said, a wide grin on her face as she removed the glass cover. She took the book out, looking it over and running her fingers lovingly over the cover. She stepped in front of the mirror and smiled down at the book and held it up to the mirror. What she said was so quiet that no sound came out, though Alice could see that her lips were moving.

The creature on the cover moved and came alive. The Queen watched the creature as if it were a pet and a gentle smile played on her lips.

"I have brought another heart," she told the creature, turning back around and holding the book in her crossed arms.

Alice fought to keep from making a sound as something darted out of the book and plunged into the White Rabbit's chest.

The White Rabbit looked more shocked than anything else. He looked down at his own chest as the thing drew out of him. The fear drained right out of his eyes, being replaced by absolutely nothing at all as it withdrew with the White

Rabbit's heart speared on the end of a single long white po
celain claw.

Alice could tell now that it was a finger of a much greater
beast contained within the book. The claw curled back and
away from the White Rabbit and brought his heart closer to
the Queen of Hearts.

"That is quite a nice heart," the Queen said, amused.
"And look at how fast it beats. No wonder you always seemed
to be in such a hurry, my dear White Rabbit." She laughed,
cruel and merciless and she placed one hand on it as if placing a finger to the lips of someone to quiet them. It seemed
to slow the beating of the heart on the claw and the Queen
breathed in deeply. When the Queen opened her eyes again,
they glowed red for only a moment before she looked to the
three still in her room.

"You are dismissed," she said. "And if you see a small
blonde girl in blue wandering around, bring her to me
immediately."

They bowed and left with the White Rabbit who had
none of his former lustre left. He looked rather like the life
had drained out of him. There was a small amount of longing
when he looked up at his heart pierced on the end of the claw,
but that was about all there was left and, as he was escorted out
of the room, even that seemed to fade away.

Alice realized that she was shaking, hands clamped over

her mouth and tears in her eyes. Pounding in her ears was her own heart, beating faster than any of the others in the room around her. It was all too much. This wasn't what Wonderland was supposed to be like. It was supposed to be fun with only threats of violence. Nothing bad was supposed to actually happen.

She couldn't bring herself to look away as the Queen of Hearts regarded her newly stolen heart with a cruel grin.

"And where am I going to put you?" she asked the heart. "We are running out of places, but there are still so many hearts that I don't yet possess. I suppose I'm just going to need to make more furniture. A nice chair for my desk, perhaps? And then a couch. Many of these hearts are quite soft enough for that."

The Queen of Hearts began to move, book in hand and heart still dangling on the end of the curled claw as the Queen walked closer to the desk. Alice panicked but couldn't bring herself to move. She couldn't even think of anywhere she could go.

She continued to watch in terror as the Queen drew closer, hoping she wouldn't look underneath it. She brought the book down and the claw lowered to pierce into the desk. When it withdrew, the White Rabbit's heart was gone and the claw went back into the book.

Alice watched as the Queen of Hearts went back to her

alter and lifted the glass cover. She placed the book carefully back in its place. "That is all for now. Don't you worry, there are still many more hearts left to collect. We've discovered a whole new land far, far away that I would rather like as well. Don't you worry, you will be kept well fed."

The Queen of Hearts stroked the book, smiling down at it with pride.

When she put the cover back over it, Alice let out a sigh of relief and slumped against the side of the desk. As she did so, her dress rubbed against the glass, a small squeak echoing in the otherwise completely silent room.

Alice stiffened and her breath caught in her throat. She dared not look to see if the Queen of Hearts had heard it. Her mind went through what few options she could think of. She could run, but her legs didn't want to move. She could eat the cake! But that would make her easier to find. Was there anything else left in her pockets? She couldn't remember.

The click of the Queen of Hearts' heels came closer and closer to the desk. Alice panicked, trying to think of anything else she could do and what she was forgetting. As the hearts beat around her, so much slower than her own, she couldn't think clearly. It was like they were getting louder.

The Queen of Hearts stopped just beside the desk, her red shoes visible between the floating hearts. Alice stayed perfectly still, barely daring to breathe, hoping that she wasn't going to check under here. Then she saw the skirt bunch up as the Queen knelt down, slowly but surely, and Alice's breath caught in her throat as the Queen finally showed herself, looking under the desk, her expression quite unimpressed.

"What do we have here?" she asked, looking at Alice with her cold eyes. "Why, it's a very rude little girl who managed to keep her head. Well, up to your feet, you should know how to greet royalty by now."

Alice felt her blood go cold as the Queen rose, slowly moving as she felt her limbs go quite numb out of fear. She didn't know what she was going to do to get out of this, only that she should greet the queen, terrified of losing her heart or no. Her manners had gotten her out of trouble last time. At least, she thought that might have been it. Fear did rather bad things to her memory.

She got up to her feet from under the desk and straightened out her uniform as well she could before dipping into a deep curtsy. "Greetings Your Majesty. I am Alice," she said.

"You are an eavesdropper now then, are you?" the Queen of Hearts asked. "No, no response needed out of you. You've been quite rude enough as it is. You should not speak. You've been spying for someone who seeks to steal back all the hearts that I've so very carefully collected. And why shouldn't I have them at all? I am the Queen of Hearts! After all that's happened, I deserve to take back what is rightfully mine. Perhaps they won't return my husband to me, but they have returned my youth and my beauty. And they've begun to set order to the chaos Wonderland once was. And really," she said, a sly grin on her face as she looked back at Alice, "isn't Wonderland one place that truly needed order and a beautiful ruler to keep it that way?"

Alice said nothing. She was still scared that the book was going to leave the case soon and her heart would soon be gone as well. She really didn't want that. She wasn't from Wonderland and she didn't think she'd still be alive after her heart was removed.

"How have you returned to Wonderland?" the Queen of Hearts asked, bending down to look Alice in the eyes. Alice stared back, almost certain there was sweat on her brow and she tried very hard to make sure she stood still without shaking. "The last we saw of you, my men tried to capture you and you vanished like that infernal cat. Well?" she snapped.

Alice jumped, her mind racing as she tried to come up with an answer. Her thoughts were starting to come together through the fear and her need to find a way to escape was coming through. She needed a little more time to think of something. She needed to stall.

"I didn't mean to come here," she said, trying very carefully to choose her words so that she wasn't lying, but didn't betray anything she might be able to use to escape. "The Cheshire Cat pushed me into a mirror and I ended up here."

The Queen of Hearts regarded her carefully, pacing around her and closer to the book. "I don't take kindly to little girls who lie to me," she said. "You wouldn't happen to be *lying* to me, would you?"

The Queen walked past the altar and the book and over to the mirror. She looked at herself, adjusting her dress just so and assuring herself that she was still just as beautiful as she thought she was. Alice watched and thought it was an awful lot like when her mother wanted to assure herself that she wasn't old yet.

"I have been told that you were wandering around the castle before now," the Queen of Hearts said, not looking at Alice. "He said that you've stolen a glass from my table, but then put it right back. I suppose you think this sets things right, but you are quite the nasty child, aren't you? Stealing, spying, doing all sorts of unsavoury things. You know, I can solve all of these nasty habits of yours."

Alice inched her way over to the altar and the book. If she could take the book, then the Queen would not have it. Without the book, the creature with its heart sealing claw wouldn't be there any longer to try and take her heart away.

"I think it would be best if I learned my lessons myself," Alice offered. She could hear her heart beating louder, faster than it was actually going and she was very certain there was something wrong about the sound of it. "I wouldn't want to trouble Your Majesty on something so trivial as myself. I am young and should try to learn my lessons myself before troubling someone so important as yourself."

The Queen looked back at her and seemed pleased with this response. "Oh, Alice dear," she said, coming over to her. Alice wasn't sure how the Queen didn't hear her heart pounding considering how loud it was getting. "What a delight you are. You seem to think that you can talk your way out of this, but you seem to already know what will happen to you, don't you? A shame, perhaps, but you will learn to accept it. I may keep you, though. I have quite fancied the idea of having a daughter."

Alice realized what the pounding was and it was not her heart. That was pounding hard and quickly, but the sound in her ears wasn't the beating of her heart but the gallop of horse hooves which were drawing nearer and nearer. Yes, she was quite the damsel in distress yet again and she could use a little saving right now.

The Queen didn't seem to hear it. If she did, she ignored it. Instead, she bent down to put her hand under Alice's chin, rising her terrified little face up so that she could lean in close and inspect it. "Well, you aren't quite as pretty as I might have liked you," she said, turning Alice's face one way, then the other. "Quite plain, really. Your hair is quite the wrong colour, this yellow, and we will find something to do about that blue in your eyes and replace it with something more fitting that matches better. But it is something to start with, I suppose. It is quite hard to make a mouse from a leaf, after all."

Alice had no time to wonder what that meant or to build up any courage to question her or even to tell her she already had a mother. At that moment, the door slammed open and the White Knight was there, lance in hand and sitting tall on his horse, the King sitting behind him.

"Ahoy! Ahoy!" he proclaimed, clearly not having taken the moment to look around him. "Check!"

The King dismounted behind him, his eyes alight as he looked around at the room of hearts, staring on in shock and horror as he moved very slowly and carefully about. The White Knight continued to stand there, seeing that his visor had blocked most of the horror away from his eyes, but he did tilt his head slightly as he looked at who he was rescuing from whom.

"Why, I say. I remember you."

The Queen of Hearts pushed Alice to one side, sending her closer to the altar and looking wildly at her two intruders. "You!" she yelled at them both, though more the White Knight who she turned on first. "I have heard you trouncing through my halls for so long, back and forth and that infernal racket intruding on my business for weeks! How did you get in here?"

"Why, I am always present when there is a damsel in distress and in need of rescuing!" he proclaimed loudly. "Though if I had known that she would be in distress quite so often as she has been, I might have insisted on keeping her closer by. Though I don't know, truly, that I might, to be honest."

Alice took the moment to get to her feet and remove the glass from the altar, dropping it to the ground with a clunk. The glass did not shatter, only dropping onto the hearts as they beat louder around it. She took the book, careful to make sure the creature on the cover didn't face her and tucked it under her shirt before she turned back.

The Queen was already facing her. "You—"

"I think not," the White King said, having moved slowly and quietly behind the Queen and grabbing her shoulder. "You have been captured. Check. You are our prisoner and you will release the hearts of Wonderland now."

The Queen of Hearts laughed then, merciless and cruel. Alice backed away as the Queen's eyes fell on her. "Do you truly think that you can capture me?" the Queen demanded. "I am the Queen of Hearts and you have entered my room! Your silly rules are not going to work here."

"Now, my lady, I think you are being quite out of line," the White Knight said. He dismounted and raised his visor to look at her directly. "We have captured you fairly. It is only right that you... my word..."

The White Knight went completely speechless as he looked about the room, not knowing what more to say or do. He stared, looking at all the hearts that lined the room. This was strangeness, but it was nothing that Wonderland was prepared to handle.

Alice backed away, stopping when she bumped into the side of the mirror. She looked from the mirror to the Queen, then back to the mirror, not sure if she'd seen right.

In the mirror, Alice saw the pond at school with Cat's tree hanging over it. The sun was shining and there were only a few people sitting under the tree.

The White Knight let out a sound of surprise and the Queen of Hearts began to laugh again. Alice snapped right back around.

Behind her, the Queen of Hearts had her hand in the White Knight's chest, the White King having taken a step back to watch the horror unfold himself. The Queen withdrew her hand and breathed deep the fumes of the heart as the White Knight went perfectly still, the life gone from his eyes and replaced with nothing at all.

"I don't think it's proper for a Queen to get her hands dirty," the Queen said, turning back to Alice. "However, there are times that I must. I must collect my hearts, after all."

Alice looked from one side to another for some way around her. "My new darling daughter, you may begin your training as a proper princess by bringing your mother her book," she said, one hand outstretched, a heart in the other.

The White King lunged forward and attempted to knock her over. It was a clumsy move at best, but it did the trick. The Queen of Hearts toppled over, the White Knight's heart skittering out of her hand and across the floor. The White Knight watched it, uncertain of what he was supposed to do now.

Alice tried to back away and tripped against the mirror. The mirror fell behind her, but she fell faster and went right through the glass.

CHAPTER 10

Cold and Wet

ALICE FELL BACK through the mirror and did not land. The next thing she saw was herself hovering for barely a second over the very still pond before falling face first into it.

She inhaled a mouthful of water and started to flail and drag herself back up to the surface. Her clothes were heavy and dragged her down as she tried desperately to get to air. Her lungs burned and she coughed, inhaling more water. She kept trying to climb back up to where the air was, but everything was starting to go dark.

The last thing she saw was a dark shadow coming closer.

ALICE WOKE TO her lungs violently coughing out the water that had gotten into them. She curled up on the grass, cold and still feeling weak. She was trembling, but still aware that there were other people around her. One of them kept patting her hard on the back as she coughed. Slowly, she started to make out their voices and their words.

"At least you remembered," one of them said.

"How did she get there?" another asked. "Did you see her?"

"Nope. You?"

"Nope. Alice? Alice, can you talk?"

Her coughing finally stopped, but she could still feel water in her lungs. She whimpered softly, her throat raw from the coughing. She looked up to see three identical faces looking back down at her and relaxed.

Mike, Mark, and Matt. She was back at Lucena Academy.

"Cold," she said hoarsely. She was freezing, her clothes feeling heavy as they clung to her. Though the sun was out, it was still November and the day was too cold for her to be soaked and lying on the grass.

It was only part of the reason she was shaking so much, though. She'd only narrowly escaped the Queen, then nearly drowned. She had been so close to ending up like the White Rabbit. Or the White Knight. Her heart could have joined theirs in the walls.

She could still hear the hearts beating. Or maybe that was her own.

They got her to sit up and she started coughing again. Her

head spun and she started to waver. Hands kept her upright and tried to get her up to her feet.

"Come on," one of them said. She felt them dragging her up to her feet. "We gotta get you inside."

She kept coughing and doubled over almost as soon as she was on her feet. She clasped her arms around her stomach and realized that the book wasn't there anymore. She looked around, panicking that she had dropped it. There was a monster in there. She couldn't let it get out.

"Where—"

She couldn't manage anything else, her lungs still trying to get rid of the water.

"It's okay, Alice," he said, trying to get her to walk. He put an arm under hers and around her back, trying to pull her along. Another one came on her other side to help. "You're going to be okay."

"The book..."

"We've got your book," he said. "Come on. You need to get inside."

She looked back and saw one of the other triplets holding the book, looking at the creature on the cover. Alice felt too weak to try and take it back, content that the creature hadn't reached out of it. It had retreated, she thought, and she leaned into the brother that held her up.

"Alice? Alice, you awake?"

"Yeah," she said weakly, stumbling along with them. It was getting easier to breathe, though she was still feeling dizzy. "Thank you."

"How did you get into the middle of the pond?" the one on her other side asked. Matt, maybe? "Were you in the tree or something?"

"And where have you been?" Mike. That one was Mike. "Addie's been freaking out."

Alice said nothing, focusing instead on trying to put one foot in front of the other. She was starting to feel a little stronger. Her breathing was less ragged and the world wasn't spinning as violently as before. Slowly, she was starting to move on her own two feet.

"Alice?" Mike asked. "You still with us?"

"Yeah," she said.

"Ask her where she got this book," Mark asked. "It's kind of freaking me out."

"It's a book," Matt said.

"Yeah, but this thing on the cover is creepy. And it's dry already."

"It's a book."

"It's a *creepy* book."

They finally got into the dorms but the warmth barely penetrated her soaking wet clothing. She was still shivering and felt like she was covered in ice. The cold was still everywhere, seeping into her head through her wet hair. She couldn't even feel her feet anymore.

"Go get Addie," Mike told Mark. "Alice is probably going to need a change of clothes, too."

Mark left and the rest of them continued to the infirmary just off the entrance hall. She'd never been through the doors and was a little surprised to find a white room with Miss Amanda sitting at the front desk instead of a receptionist. She looked up when the door opened.

"Alice?" she said, coming around the desk. Her attention turned to the boys carrying her. "What did you do?"

"Nothing!" Matt said. "Why do you always think it's our fault?"

"You'd think you wanted us to leave her drowning in the pond."

"We need to get you dry," Miss Amanda said, shaking her head at the boys and pulling Alice away. "One of you find Adrianna."

"Already taken care of," Matt told her. "She should be here in a minute."

Miss Amanda grabbed a few towels and a change of clothes and led Alice to one of the beds slowly, noticing that she was still a bit unsteady on her feet. "Dry off and change into this," she told her. "I'll get the doctor. She'll be with you in a minute, okay?"

Alice nodded and Miss Amanda drew the curtains around her. The clothes consisted of white pants and a white shirt, both of which looked a little big for her. Not that she cared right now. She stripped, each item of clothing falling to the ground with a slushy thump. She felt warmer after she changed, though her head was still aching from the cold. She started to towel off her hair when the doctor appeared.

"Alice?" the woman asked. "Are you ready?"

"Yes," Alice said, taking a seat on the bed. She stopped trying to dry her hair.

"Hello," the doctor said. She was an short woman in her forties with kind eyes. "I'm Doctor Wong. What happened?"

"I fell in the pond," Alice said, carefully cutting out anything that had to do with Wonderland. "And I tried to swim, but I can't. And then everything went really dark and I woke up and I was coughing on the grass."

Doctor Wong was already shining a light in her eyes and checking her heart rate with the stethoscope. "And why did you fall in the pond?"

Alice hesitated. She didn't have an answer to that yet. She'd only just been in Wonderland. She'd nearly died twice in the past hour. Her head was still spinning too much to come up with anything. Doctor Wong put something around her arm and it began to tighten.

"It's okay if you don't want to say," Doctor Wong said, smiling. "How are you feeling now?"

"Cold," Alice said, feeling a wave of relief that she wasn't going to press. "I don't feel like coughing as much anymore, but I'm still really dizzy."

"When was the last time you ate?"

"I..." Alice couldn't remember. Middle wish pie, a treacle tart, some water, a bit of cake and nibble of mushroom. She didn't want to say anything about that, though.

Doctor Wong nodded and took the thing off of her arm. "Into bed," she said. Alice got under the covers and Doctor Wong put a thermometer in her mouth. "Keep this under your tongue. I'll be right back. I just need a word with Miss Amanda."

Alice nodded and sank into the pillow. A wave of exhaustion washed over her. She felt like she'd been running for so long and now, now she had a break. Her eyelids were getting heavy and, though she tried to keep them open, sleep took her.

WHEN SHE OPENED her eyes, there was nothing but purple. Blearily, she blinked and tried to bring up a hand to wipe at her eyes, but found it pinned down to her side. She tugged at it and managed to pull it free with a bit of a grunt, and wiped the sleep from her eyes. When she looked again, the purple took the shape of a cat with a very wide grin smiling in her face.

Alice jumped and pushed herself up, forcing the cat to stumble back down to her lap. "You," she growled at him.

"Back, I see," he said, looking at her with amusement. "I trust your heart is still in its proper place as well? Very difficult to live without one of those in these parts."

"You pushed me!"

"I did no such thing," the Cheshire Cat said, pacing back and forth on her lap. "I was merely walking. You fell. It is impolite to accuse someone of something they did not do."

"It's also impolite to not warn someone that she is being sent into danger."

"What is an adventure without a little danger?"

"A little? The Hatter is madder than ever, the March Hare is.... I don't know what happened to him. I was kidnapped by the Red Knight. I was thrown in jail. I saw the Queen of Hearts use a book to take the White Rabbit's heart, then she took one with her bare hands! And the room, all those hearts..."

"But you are unharmed. Perhaps you were in no real danger at all."

"At least I got the book away from her," Alice said. "but

if she can just take them herself, I don't know what good it does."

"You got the book?" he asked, a purr lacing his words. "Good of you. There isn't nearly enough reading happening any longer. Books are meant for reading, you see. A book unread is nothing more than a pile of paper with a binding, though in this case it is quite a nice binding. I do not see it here, though. It is not good to leave books out of reach. Especially not that one."

Alice swiped at him. "Stop talking like that and give me a straight answer," she demanded, voice not raising, but very determined.

"Another time, perhaps," he said, skipping back away from her arm. With each trot backwards, a little more of him disappeared until only his eyes lingered for a moment longer and he was gone.

"Damn cat," Alice cursed, falling back on the bed. Her mind was swimming with questions and she wanted answers to them all. Things like why did he trip her and did he know what was going on over there? How had she gotten back? And why did she have to come back through the lake instead of a mirror?

"Alice?"

Alice sat back up on the bed, eyes darting around the small curtained room that gave her privacy. She was suddenly aware that someone might have heard her outside of these curtains and her heart dropped. No, no one was supposed to know. Not here.

She saw Adrianna peeking in between two of the sheets. Eyes wide and watching the spot that the Cheshire Cat had vanished from. Her eyes trailed slowly up to Alice, like she couldn't even believe her eyes.

"Alice?" she asked again. "Who were you talking to?"

Alice tried to think of an explanation, but she couldn't come up with anything. "No one," she said.

"I thought I saw something there," she said, coming closer to Alice's bedside. "And I heard someone else."

"You were probably just imagining it."

Adrianna took a seat on the small chair by her bed, shaking her head. "You said something about a Queen of Hearts and a hatter and a hare and a white rabbit. And there was definitely someone else here. I heard him. Does... does this have to do with that Wonderland place? Is it real?"

Alice didn't move a muscle, her eyes fixated on Adrianna. "How do you know about Wonderland?"

Adrianna bit her lip and looked down. She took a deep breath before looking back up imploringly at Alice, words falling quickly out of her mouth. "I'm sorry, I didn't mean to read it, but you always left your journal open and I've been having so much trouble coming up with things to write for

English so I've been peeking at yours. You already help me so much with the rest of it. I didn't want to bug you more. I wanted to tell you earlier because everything about Wonderland sounded really cool, but you never wanted to talk about it and… and I don't know. I'm sorry."

Adrianna looked down at the bed as Alice continued looking at her. She read it. She knew. Her father would find out that she'd been thinking about Wonderland or worse, find out that she'd been back. She'd be brought home and sent to the doctors and never be allowed out ever again. It was over. Everything.

"It's just a story," she said weakly. It was her last hope. "I made it all up."

"Really?" Adrianna asked.

"Yeah. And I was probably just talking in my sleep. And you probably just saw something in the light. Wonderland isn't real."

Adrianna fell silent, looking back down at the bed. Alice watched her for a long moment, desperately hoping that Adrianna believed her lies.

"So are you mad at me?" Adrianna asked. "You know. For reading it."

"No." Alice couldn't believe it. She bought it? If she was willing to accept it was all a story and wasn't going to tell anyone about it, she was willing to forgive her for anything else she might have done. "Just promise you won't tell anyone."

"I won't!" Adrianna said, brightening up. "I promise I won't tell anyone. It is really cool, though."

"How long have I been sleeping?" Alice asked, not quite meeting Adrianna's eyes.

"Since this morning," Adrianna said. "Mark came by soaking wet and said they found you drowning in the pond and you were down here. I was supposed to go get Miss Amanda if you woke up. She wanted to know how you got there. She thinks my brothers had something to do with it."

Alice smiled to herself. It hadn't been that long she was gone, at least.

"But you've been gone all weekend," Adrianna continued. "Where were you?"

"All weekend?" Alice looked back up at Adrianna. "What day is it?"

"Sunday."

It was Friday night when the Cheshire Cat tripped her into the mirror. She'd been gone so much longer than last time, though it felt like she'd done so much less. And Miss Amanda wanted to question her about what had happened, no less. Her mind began turning, trying to think of some reason why she might have been missing for a day on top of drowning.

"Joe told me not to tell anyone you were gone, though," Adrianna continued after a moment. "He said that you probably just got lost and that everyone would keep an eye out for you."

"Oh. Yeah. I just got really lost." Alice wasn't sure why Adrianna's brothers were covering for her so much, but she was going to have to thank them. She wasn't even going to have to come up with her own lies this time.

"Awake, I see," Doctor Wong said from the part in the curtain. "And feeling better. Adrianna, I believe you were supposed to go find someone."

Adrianna left to go find Miss Amanda, Doctor Wong smiling at Alice. "How are you feeling?" she asked, getting out the thermometer.

"A lot better," Alice said.

"Well, it looks like we've avoided hypothermia at least," she said, putting the thermometer into Alice's mouth and checking the rest of her. "Your blood pressure is still pretty low. And your temperature is quite high. I think you're going to have to stay for a little longer. We'll get you some dinner at least. Do you think you can keep it down?"

Alice nodded.

"Good. Now that you're out of danger, you're also going to need to wash off. There's a shower in the back with towels and a clean change of clothing. Once you're done, we'll get you fed and you should rest."

"Okay," Alice said, getting out of bed. She was much steadier on her feet now, though she still felt weak. Doctor Wong showed her the way, watching her until she was sure Alice could handle it on her own.

Cat was right. Wonderland wasn't the same place of fun and games it once was. Already it had taken its toll on her.

CHAPTER 11

Sick Day

ALICE DIDN'T SEE Miss Amanda until late the next morning. She came in with breakfast and several books, smiling as she settled down next to her. She set breakfast down on the side table and started looking for the tray Alice could use as a table. "How are you feeling?" she asked.

"Much better, thank you," Alice said. Her mind was spinning. She knew what was coming and she hadn't thought of a reason for falling in the pond yet.

"The boys told me what happened," Miss Amanda said, placing the tray of food across her lap and nodding to Alice to eat.

"Thank you," Alice said. She started eating, hoping that the food might give her some inspiration. At the very least, maybe if she kept her mouth full Miss Amanda wouldn't be able to ask her anything.

"They said they dared you to go up into the tree and you fell. It was an accident. Is this true?"

She couldn't believe it. They lied for her? She didn't know why they did it, but she'd have to thank them eventually. "Yeah," she said after swallowing her waffles. "I just lost my grip. I used to be really good at climbing trees, though, so I thought it would be okay. They aren't in trouble, are they?"

Miss Amanda smiled. "Not this time," she said. "It sounds like it really was an accident. Maybe stay away from the pond until you learn to swim, though, okay?"

Alice laughed, a little embarrassed, and finished her waffles. Once she was done, Miss Amanda brought out the books, one for each of the classes she was going to miss that day, and the assignments for the day.

Though she knew she could stop whenever she wanted — Miss Amanda more than willing to let her take a break — Alice was quick to get to work on all of her homework. Miss Amanda was there to help if she needed it, but she didn't have any trouble with her classes yet. It was still stuff she had covered with her tutor at home.

When Doctor Wong came to check her in the afternoon, she proclaimed that Alice was free to go, but would need to take it easy. She wrote a note for Alice to miss gym for the next week and advised her to stay indoors for a while before sending her on her way.

Alice changed into the uniform Adrianna had brought her before she left the infirmary and Miss Amanda escorted her up to her room before leaving.

No one had gotten back from classes yet, so Alice went to sit at her desk. She didn't have any music to listen to. Maybe for Christmas this year, she could ask her parents for a music player too, so she could have something to listen to when she was alone. She didn't know what she would do until everyone got back. Maybe read a little.

In the silence, she heard something soft, but it grew louder. A pulse. The rhythmic beating.

The hearts.

She stopped in the middle of the room, looking around to assure herself that she wasn't really back there. No, she was still in the dorms, with Adrianna's stuff on one side and hers on the other. Bed. Desk. Mirror that showed a familiar smoking caterpillar looking quite worried.

She tore her eyes off the mirror and forced herself to sit down at the desk. She was not seeing this. She wasn't hearing anything. She was still recovering from the hypothermia and she was still very tired.

Or maybe she needed to get Wonderland out of her head again before it boiled over. If she wrote it out, it might stop. Like last time.

She looked down at her desk and found two things she

wasn't expecting. One was that there was another notebook on her old one. This one had the school's logo on it and looked brand new. It even had a small lock on it and a key sitting on top to open it.

The other was a brown, leather bound book sitting alone on the shelf above her desk. She felt like something grabbed her heart and squeezed it when she looked at it. She wanted to check to see that it was the same one, but the memory of that claw coming out of it still felt too fresh for her to want to touch it again.

Her head was starting to pound with the sound of the beating hearts rattling her brain. Wonderland had followed her out and didn't want her to just forget about it this time. It was demanding she remember and she couldn't afford to do that. One slip-up would be all it took.

She looked down at the new notebook and knew what she had to do. Taking out a pen, she started writing down everything that had happened this year. Every incident with Cat. Leaving in the middle of the night. The Mad Hatter and the Dormouse. If she got it all out, it might stop. She hoped it would stop.

She'd just started her encounter with Humpty Dumpty when the door opened.

"Alice! You're back!"

Alice looked up from the notebook and saw Adrianna

rushing over to her. She stood and let Adrianna hug her, returning it herself. She was feeling better after writing that much. She could handle a break.

"So you like the book?" Adrianna asked, looking down to see Alice had already started. "I promise I won't read this one. It's got a lock on it and everything!"

Alice laughed. "Thank you," she said. "It's won... it's great."

"You want to take a break and come for dinner? Everyone was wondering why you missed class today."

"Yeah," Alice said, closing the notebook and putting the lock on it. It clicked shut and Alice pocketed the keys. "I'm starving."

They met their friends in the Dining Hall. Sarah, Heather and Robert were deeply immersed in conversation when they joined with their dinner, Kevin rolling his eyes and attempting to shuffle away from all of them. Alice didn't make out any of the conversation, which shifted when she and Adrianna sat down.

"You're alive," Kevin said with a grin. "Welcome back."

"We heard what happened," Sarah said.

"Really?" Alice asked, her fork stopping half way to her mouth. Her mind started running through who could have possibly told them about Wonderland, but she said nothing.

"Yeah," Sarah said. "That Cat guy really has a thing for you."

Alice lowered her fork back to the plate. "What?"

"He threw her out of a tree," Kevin said.

"What?"

"Guys always do stupid stuff when they like a girl."

Alice looked to Adrianna, wide eyed and confused. That wasn't what she heard earlier. Didn't Adrianna's brothers confess to daring her up into a tree that she fell out of? When did she get thrown out of it?

Adrianna smiled weakly and went back to her dinner.

"So what's with you and him anyway?" Heather asked, turning to Alice.

"What?" Alice asked, snapping around to her, feeling like she'd just been caught by the Queen of Hearts stealing her treacle. "What do you mean?"

Sarah sighed dramatically and rolled her eyes. "You're the only one anyone's ever seen him talking to," she said. "He just ignores everyone else. No one even knows who he is. But he talks to you."

"He's an old friend from when I was little," Alice said automatically. It wasn't a lie, but Alice didn't meet her eyes when she said it. Her mind was racing, trying to prepare for the next question. She pinched the inside of her wrist, but it was never a dream.

"So you do know him!"

"She obviously knows him if she talks to him," Heather said. "Really, Sarah, do you want to do this now? She just got out of the hospital."

Sarah deflated, sitting back in her seat and saying nothing more. Alice was grateful, feeling that grip on her heart loosen a little as she went back to dinner. She found that she wasn't that hungry, but tried to eat as much as she could anyway.

Through the rest of dinner and until they walked back to the dorms, Alice stayed quiet, hoping that Sarah would not pick up the conversation again. She didn't have any more explanation as to how she knew Cat yet. Lying meant she needed to come up with a full explanation in her head that she could go back to and she wasn't ready for that yet. She could barely keep from thinking about the beating hearts still, much less come up with how she knew a disappearing cat from Wonderland that was now posing as a student.

Once they got back to their room, Alice shut the door and let out the breath she didn't realize she was holding. She felt a wave of relief knowing that she was safe from more questioning from Sarah, at least until tomorrow. Maybe she could avoid the questions for longer than that if she was careful.

"Alice?" Adrianna asked, uncertain. She shifted a little, her eyes not quite rising past Alice's feet. "How do you know Cat?"

Alice dropped onto her bed, her mind racing. *No*, she pleaded. *Not you too.*

"It's just— I was really worried," she said. "I woke up and you were just gone. And that Cat guy said that stuff about giving you something for your half birthday. And Sarah said that you were obviously secretly dating him and probably went off with him in the middle of the night and—"

"I am *not* dating that Cat!" Alice burst out. "Why would I? He's a jerk and he pushed me and —" she realized what she was about to say and quickly changed course "— and it nearly killed me! Sarah doesn't know what she's talking about."

Adrianna smiled at that, keeping her laugh in. "But you're better now, right? No more leaving in the middle of the night?"

The guilt struck Alice all at once. She was worried that Adrianna had missed her when she woke up, but she hadn't said anything yet. "I'm sorry I left like that," Alice said. "I really am. I'll try not to do it again."

"At least leave a note next time," Adrianna said.

"Okay."

Alice got ready for bed and curled up under the covers while Adrianna stayed up, trying to get homework for the next day done for the next hour before going to bed herself. Alice felt a little bad for not helping and pretending to sleep, but she felt exhausted and didn't want anyone else to ask her how she knew Cat.

By eleven Alice still couldn't sleep. Her tired mind couldn't come up with anything, but it wasn't willing to sleep yet either. She was tired and her mind kept cycling through her first encounter with Cat in Wonderland, imagining him instead as the purple haired student talking to her instead of a cat.

Her mind drifted to a few nights ago and Wonderland. Her desire for answers returned. She wanted to know why he sent her there and what he wanted. It couldn't have been to fix everything. Wonderland let her leave without doing that. She had only barely managed to save herself at the end, and only because the Queen was busy with the White Knight.

In the back of her mind, she could still hear the soft beating of thousands of hearts.

"Afraid of your dreams?" a sly voice asked.

Alice shot straight up and looked around, looking back up to the shelf above her desk where a purple cat sat, looking at the only book there and not touching it.

"And do call me Cat, if you will," he requested. "It is what I am and it is the name you have given me." He grinned widely at her, Alice feeling some of the fear melt away into a mixture of annoyance and anger. This would be so much easier if he was just a boy all the time.

"What are you doing here, Cat?" she asked. She knew he wouldn't leave her alone, but she could still get answers out of him.

"Why are any of us here really?" Cat asked, chuckling a little to himself and jumping down onto the bed. "How is Wonderland? You've seen it in its brightest days and now in its darkest nights. Is it still the wondrous place you remembered so fondly for so long?"

Alice glared at him. "Maybe you should go back there and see for yourself just how Wonderland has changed."

"I think not," Cat said. "Though it seems Wonderland may have changed you a touch and for the better. You've taken something rather important from someone rather important, I see, and you don't seem to be terribly bothered by the act itself. It seems there is a little thief in you after all."

"Why did you send me back to Wonderland?"

Cat jumped down and studied her in the dim light as if she had asked where babies came from, with enough discomfort that his grin wavered away for a moment and the sparkle left his eyes.

Good, Alice thought. Let him worry a little. After what he'd put her through, he deserved it.

"Wonderland stopped making sense," he said. "By which I mean that it started making another kind of sense that none of us were familiar with. When we tried to make it make our kind of sense, the sense of it made worse sense than ever and its sense spread much more sensibly, by which I mean by stripping us of our sense. If that makes sense."

"It doesn't."

He looked a little sad for a moment, but that passed soon enough, his eyes back with their twinkle and his grin on his face. "So tell me what you found in Wonderland this time. Any lovely treats along the way before the horrible ending?"

She was going to snap at him when she remembered something. "Middle wish pie," she said. "Hatter dropped it on me and I ate some of it. Does it do anything?"

"It's best not to worry over things that you may never know," Cat told her. "Your very middle wish is never as important as your most or least desired. In all likelihood, it was for something you likely won't even notice."

"I hope so."

"If that is all, then Wonderland has quite changed," Cat said and he jumped back up to the shelf where the book was. He sniffed it and Alice was almost certain that he hissed at it, though it was so low that she couldn't be sure. "You've done a service, though. The book is out of the Queen's clutches."

"She doesn't need the book anymore," Alice said, though she was worried. Mostly because Cat seemed to be speaking plainly. "She can do it with her own hands now."

"This book," he said, still careful not to touch it, though he came close, "is not from Wonderland. It smells of somewhere else that's much more sinister. Whatever possessed it to invade Wonderland will not stop until it's collected all the madness for itself. And then it will move to another land. And another."

"The Queen of Hearts did mention that there was somewhere else with more hearts she wanted to take," Alice said.

The Cat shook his head. "The madness of Wonderland comes from the hearts of Wonderland. If she goes elsewhere, she's going to be pulling out ordinary hearts and there is nothing at all that she can do with regular hearts. She won't be able to do anything once she gets out of Wonderland."

"I don't know if that's a good thing," Alice noted.

"It's a fine thing for Wonderland," Cat said. "It's a good thing that you've taken the book, in any case. It means she can't learn any more tricks."

"The book teaches more tricks?" Alice asked, looking at it again.

Cat nodded, but said nothing further on the matter, glaring at the book for a long moment before looking right back at Alice. "I hope you feel better, Alice," he said, sounding sincere, though a little mischievous. "You have to watch the book now. Make sure the things inside it don't get out."

He slunk away then, leaving her to lie there and look at

the book. She stared at the book a little more and opted to put it under her mattress before drifting off to sleep, feeling like she had fewer answers now than before.

CHAPTER 12

Part Treacle

EVERYTHING WAS QUIET for a while. Alice kept looking over her shoulder for something strange to happen, but nothing did. Cat seemed to have disappeared in the cold weather, even vanishing from his tree as the rain set in. It started to snow late in November, meaning that the girls were now allowed to wear pants in the cold weather along with the longer sweaters.

Alice checked to make sure the book was between her mattresses every morning and night as a routine. She'd moved it so it was on the side closest to the wall now so that she could check without Adrianna knowing and Adrianna had, mercifully, not asked her any more questions about that day or Cat.

Alice was just glad he had disappeared. When he vanished, Sarah briefly insisted that Alice broke his heart when he pushed her out of the tree, but soon dropped all of her speculation. Alice managed to get away without having to come up with some story about how she knew him, which was good because she never came up with an explanation.

Nothing odd happened until one fair snowy evening when the threat of finals were beginning to settle into their minds. They were a little late to dinner, having gotten distracted by studying. They were not the last, but the options for dinner were getting very slim when they got there.

She grabbed a plate of salad and another one of some overcooked beef and potatoes, ignoring the rose garden with chattering flowers reflected in the glass. She'd gotten used to it now. The images appeared in every reflection, but if she ignored them they eventually faded away.

Alice didn't have any issue with the slim selection until they got to the dessert section.

"There's only treacle tart left?" Alice asked, remembering the last treacle tart she ate less than fondly. There were several plates out and ready for them to take, but Alice was reluctant to take one. There were students she had passed that had cupcakes, and all that was left was a treat she had once been put on trial for stealing and once eaten while in prison.

"I've never had treacle tart," Adrianna said, taking one and putting it on her tray.

Alice didn't look as she took her plate, wishing that she

one of those chocolate cupcakes instead. Her eyes wandered out to a boy who did have one and she watched as something very weird happened while he wasn't looking. A hand appeared out of thin air and took his cupcake, drawing back and disappearing with it. When she looked back, she saw her own hand placing a chocolate cupcake on her tray.

Alice said nothing, stopping in line until Adrianna pushed her to the end. They offered their student cards, which were swiped in exchange for payment, before going to one of the empty tables. Alice kept staring down at her plate and, as she heard a yell of surprise from the boy who once had the chocolate cupcake, she felt a tinge of guilt over it. Not too much, though. She really didn't want that treacle tart.

She set her tray down, still staring oddly at the cupcake when Adrianna set hers down. "Adrianna?" she asked. "Did you see any cupcakes left when you went to get your dessert?"

"No."

"Huh," Alice said, still looking down at her plate. Adrianna's eyes followed hers and she saw the chocolate cupcake sitting on Alice's plate. She stared at it for a minute too, looking back at the options they had for dessert and then around the room as if looking for a free cupcakes table she missed.

"Where did you get that cupcake from?" Adrianna asked.

"I don't know," Alice said. She pinched the inside of her wrist. Still not dreaming. Her mind was racing. She needed to try it again, to see if it was really her doing it or if she just happened to grab one that they had missed.

But she couldn't let Adrianna know. She might ask questions. "Did you want one?"

"Sure," Adrianna said.

"Give me your tart," Alice said. "I'm going to turn it into a cupcake."

Alice looked around until she saw another chocolate cupcake sitting on another plate a few tables over. She took Adrianna's plate and held it just under the table. Her eyes on the cupcake plate, she moved both of her hands forward under the table, both of her hands appearing by the cupcake. She set the tart plate down and picked up the chocolate cupcake. With a deep breath, she withdrew her hands quickly and pulled them back above the table.

She was holding a plate with a chocolate cupcake on it in her formerly empty hand and nothing where the treacle tart had been.

Adrianna had her eyes open wide watching and Alice wasn't sure what to say as she set down the cupcake. "You're a magician!" she said. "I didn't know you knew how to do magic tricks! Can you tell me how you did it? That was amazing."

"Well," Alice said, starting on her own food to avoid finishing. Adrianna seemed to understand what she was doing and she went back to her own plate, Alice hoping that she would forget the whole thing.

She had thought she left all that food that she'd eaten in Wonderland, or at least their maddening effects. It had been over a week. Surely there wouldn't be any sign of that tart left in her system.

She thought more on it as the meal passed and she finally ended at the cupcake. She stared at it, trying to make sense of what was happening to her. Was this permanent? Had she really gained that annoying habit of appearing and disappearing like the Cheshire Cat had forever? Could something from Wonderland have actually made it here?

Did this mean she could finally prove Wonderland existed?

Alice decided to eat it. There was no reason to try convincing anyone that Wonderland was real. She'd learned her lesson. She would continue to pretend that Wonderland was all in her imagination. She needed to concentrate on her school work and passing her finals so that she could come back next semester. And she needed to keep not talking about Wonderland so that she wouldn't be sent back to the doctors again.

On the other hand, if she could actually do everything she could in Wonderland, it would help should Cat ever try to push her into Wonderland again. Maybe it would even help her get out. If she could just want herself elsewhere, then she could want herself back to her room.

Adrianna seemed to forget about it all over the course of the meal anyway, though she did look at Alice like she had suddenly grown rabbit ears from her head band. She had to brush her hair back with her hands before she was able to assure herself that there was nothing there.

As they went back to their room, Alice felt a chill run through her, but told herself it was the wind. The pit of her stomach and her instincts tried to tell her otherwise, but she went up to study with the others anyway.

Throughout the evening, she continued to test the limits of her treacle abilities a little more, pulling books out from her bag that were sitting on her shelf in her room and putting them back when she was done. No one seemed to notice, but she made sure to be the last one to leave so no one would notice she had an empty bag at the end of the night.

When she finally got back to her room, Adrianna wasn't awake. It was a bit of a relief. Alice went to the notebook that Adrianna had left her and wrote a new section for today, chronicling her discovery of what she could now do. It didn't make sense.

She knew full well that Wonderland had left a lingering effect on her this time. She wasn't quite sure what to make of it. She wasn't sure how she'd gone quite so long without noticing it until now. As she wrote, she started to wonder what else would be coming back to haunt her.

The tart still affecting her bothered her more, though. Could all of her move? She didn't want to try it just yet. She was only just getting used to her hands going away from her and she wasn't quite ready to handle all of her moving. Still, she was a little worried that she was now permanently part treacle. What else was going to happen to her? What else did she have in Wonderland that might also spring back up?

The middle wish pie hadn't done anything to her yet, at least. Not that she knew of, anyway. Maybe it was a wish for her to pass all of her classes. If that were the case, then there would be nothing to worry about, but Wonderland was a bit of a selfish place and it would probably end up being something to do with it. Alice didn't know what it would be, but she wasn't looking forward to finding out.

She reached a hand down the side of her bed again, feeling carefully and finally breathing a sigh of relief. The book was still there. That book was going to be more trouble than anything else. She knew that somehow. The Cat may have vanished, but she knew he'd be back to find out what was in the book soon enough and when that happened, she would pull a water gun from somewhere on campus and squirt him right between the eyes before he got close to it.

Something about the book had driven the Queen of Hearts mad, and she worried that it was going to draw in Cat and make him do the same thing. He was far too interested in it already.

Alice finally drifted off to sleep, though not after thinking of several more ways she would use her disappearing hands to pull something else from seeming nowhere and smack Cat back down and out of her way first. She was part treacle now. She might as well find some way to enjoy that.

Her dream was a restful one. She dreamed she was in a beautiful gown and walking through the snow of the school, looking around the ground for something. She wasn't sure what, but it was imperative she find it. Still, she wasn't too worried about finding whatever it was. There was enough left over that she didn't have to worry about it.

Shifting about in the snow was a small rabbit with a pocket watch made out of carrots. He nibbled at it as Alice drew closer and closer to it, just a normal rabbit nibbling away at a pocket watch made out of carrot. He looked up at her, eyes wide and fearful for a moment, then calmer as Alice stopped and bent down to get a better look at him.

"I used to be late," he told her. "I dressed well and I was always late. I don't have to worry about any of that now."

Alice wasn't sure what that meant, but she reached out a hand and pet him. She stroked his soft fur once, then twice, the rabbit nuzzling into her hand as she did so. On the third stroke, he became a little bunny sculpture made out of snow.

When Alice stood up, she was in a whole garden like that. It was a garden where everything was made of snow. There was an egg falling off a wall, flowers, the dormouse in a rather large coffee pot and a shattered clock. The Dormouse shivered a little, though, the only thing besides Alice that moved and shook the snow off of his coat. He reached back into the tea pot and pulled out a top hat, placing it above his head and letting it fall over his eyes. Once it did, snow started to cover him again, but there was no snow falling from the sky.

Alice walked over to him, curious and uncertain about what was going on, but she was fairly certain that she was lost. "Pardon me," Alice said. "Do you know what I'm looking for? I've lost it and I must get it back."

The Dormouse shook again, the snow falling off of him. "I am missing the head for my hat," the Dormouse informed her. "It ran away to look for hair. I cannot find it."

"If I find that, will you help me?" Alice asked.

"No," the Dormouse said.

Alice kept walking down the path and into the school that appeared on the other side of the garden. There were many people there, some of them in strange costumes and some in regular clothes and some that weren't people so much as playing cards with nothing written on them. She didn't quite know what it was, but she had to keep looking for something.

"You shouldn't go that way," someone said, but when she

turned around she was alone in the room. "It won't end well if you go that way."

"But I must find it," Alice insisted to no one at all. "I must!"

"Just don't go that way," the voice said.

"But I know it's over here." And she did know that. She didn't know how, but it didn't matter. She needed to get it and she didn't know how long it would take to get there, but she needed to get that thing she was looking for. She had to return it to someone important. There was something she needed to do with it.

Alice went up the stairs, certain that something she needed to do was up here. She followed up the stairs further and further, the windows floating to either side and showing bits of red outside and things flying past them. Alice didn't stop to look, though, no matter what the things at the window said and how they asked. Even the very sad bird asking what it was going to do. She ignored it. She needed to be somewhere and, while she wanted to help, she just didn't know what to do.

When she reached the top of the stairs, there was a beautiful queen standing there with no face. She regarded Alice and Alice remembered her manners. She knelt down into a deep curtsy. "My queen," she said, not looking up as the Queen approached her. There was a low beating that began around her, but Alice thought that might have been her own heart.

She was supposed to fetch something for the queen, but she hadn't found it yet. She'd come back too soon.

"Alice, where is my book?" she asked, her voice cold, like she was ready to snap into a much more evil form. "Have you found me my book yet?"

"Not yet, my queen," she said, not looking up from her curtsy. "I have been looking everywhere. I shall find it soon, I promise."

The queen was quiet a long moment. "Do find it, child," she said, her voice suddenly very gentle. She paced around Alice. "When you fetch me my book, then you can become my princess and we shall do many great things together. All the people will be helped, but first we need that book. You understand, of course."

"Yes, my queen," she said, finally rising. She was alone again, but the room seemed to be alive, pulsing around her and there were silent screams echoing from every direction, like the pain and suffering of several creatures were crying out.

Something felt weird about all this. She was going to be a princess. There should be none of this fear or creatures crying in pain. It felt wrong.

Alice pinched the inside of her wrist and felt the world around her break. A dream. It was only a dream.

It was still dark and she was still very tired. Alice knew

she'd only been asleep for a couple hours, but there was something bothering her. More specifically, there was something physically that felt very wrong. Like something was...

There was something moving on her bed, something rather large and crawling there. Gasping, she shot up in her bed and let out a yelp, realizing that the thing on her bed was a very large purple cat.

"What—Why—You!" she stuttered as she reached under her pillow and pulled out the first thing that she could think of, a water gun. In the morning she would be more concerned about how much that seemed like second nature to her, but for the moment she only hoped it was full as she shot it at Cat.

The water hit him between the eyes and he hissed, recoiling at it and then snapping forward. He pinned Alice with one paw on her shoulder to keep her down, and the other paw threatening her with the claws out and pointing dangerously close to Alice's face.

Alice stared at the claws, eyes wide and breath caught in her throat as she pressed herself into the pillow. His claws on her shoulder dug painfully into her skin.

"That was terribly rude of you, girl," he hissed at her, lingering there for a moment before retracting and stepping back. Alice breathed a sigh of relief, but continued to watch the Cheshire Cat as she sat up.

"What are you doing here?" Alice noted, rubbing gently at her shoulder that he had sunk his claws into. "Going to try and push me into another mirror again?"

"I'm here for that book," the Cheshire Cat said, pacing back and forth along her bed. He finally settled, sitting on her legs and staring at her.

"It's being taken care of," Alice said. "No one from Wonderland is going to find it. The Queen of Hearts isn't going to get it back. You don't need to worry about anything. You can go away and never come back and find someone else to annoy."

The Cheshire Cat's eyes bore into her, leaning forward threateningly. Alice didn't back down, too tired and foultempered to put up with his games. Finally, his eyes seemed to catch on something else and he eased off of her as he followed it for a moment before looking back to Alice.

"I hadn't expected that you would keep it hidden away," he said. "Children are meant to be curious creatures, seeking out adventure. You sought out Wonderland and were curious enough to find out what happened since you left. I'd thought you would at the very least read the book when you found it."

"Well, I'm not going to," Alice said flatly. "You can leave now."

"I think not," the Cheshire Cat said. "I must know what is in the book to drive the Queen of Hearts mad."

"The Queen of Hearts was always mad," Alice told him. "Inside the book is a monster that steals hearts. Curiosity solved. Let me go back to sleep."

"I think not."

Something in her mind clicked, a piece falling into place. Alice rubbed her face, trying to wake up a little more. It couldn't be right. "Don't tell me you sent me to Wonderland just so that I could steal the book and read it for you. How would you even know I'd find it and come back with it?"

"Stop your questioning!" Cheshire Cat pounced on Alice, pinning her again. His claws scratched into her shoulder and she stifled a whimper as she tried to shrink away from the claws once more in her face. "I want to see that book! You will tell me where it is!"

"Alice?"

Alice looked over to where Adrianna was waking up, pushing herself up and brushing at her bleary eyes. She looked over and seemed to be in shock for a moment, freezing at the scene before her eyes.

Alice realized that Cheshire Cat had gotten a bit heavier on top of her. His claws had become larger and were no longer digging into her flesh.

Adrianna let out a very loud, piercing scream.

Alice grinned as she looked back up at the Cheshire Cat,

who was now in the form of a boy. "You might want to leave now," Alice told him. "Miss Amanda will be here any minute and you don't want to get caught, do you?"

Cat let out a hiss before disappearing much more quickly than Alice had ever seen him go. Her heart, she only just realized, was pounding. She sat carefully back up, her hand slipping under her bed and between the mattresses to assure herself that there was nothing to worry about. The book was still there and she felt a wave of relief pass over her.

She got up out of bed and went to Adrianna's. "It's okay," Alice said. "Calm down, everything's okay."

Adrianna stopped screaming as Alice settled on her bed, staring at her in shock. She dove at her, hugging her and pulling back. "Are you okay? What happened?"

"I'm fine," Alice said. She turned back to see that the door was opening behind them and quickly whispered to Adrianna, "Just follow my lead, okay?"

Miss Amanda was in the doorway, wearing pyjama pants and an oversized shirt. She looked a bit frantic, her eyes darting back and forth, relaxing when she saw it was just the two of them. "What happened?" she asked.

"Just a bad dream," Alice said quickly, Adrianna still seeming to have not recovered yet. "We'll be okay."

"All right," Miss Amanda said, nodding absently. "If either of you need me, just knock." She left, closing the door softly behind her. Alice could hear a few voices in the hall and went to lock the door before going back to sit next to Adrianna.

Adrianna slowly started to calm down, though she still seemed to be having trouble with whatever she'd just seen. "What happened?" she asked finally. "I heard something and woke up and there was you and Cat was there and it looked like he was threatening you or something and—"

"It's okay," Alice insisted. "Cat's gone. Everything's alright."

"But *where* did he go?" Adrianna asked. "What did he want? He seemed so mad."

"I..."

"What's going on, Alice?" Adrianna pressed. "Who is he? Were you going to disappear again?"

"I wasn't... I'm *not*..."

"You can tell me what's happening. I won't even tell anyone, I promise. I don't even care if you are dating him, I just—"

"I am not dating him!" Alice snapped.

"Then what's going on?"

Alice hesitated. Adrianna still looked terrified and the guilt of lying to her was doubled looking at her.

With a deep sigh, Alice rose to her feet and went to her desk. She picked up the notebook and unlocked it. She stood there for a minute staring at it, taking a few deep breaths and trying to figure out if she was really going to do this.

It took her every ounce of effort to turn back around. Her feet felt like they were made of lead and she had to force every step. She was going to regret this. She might never be able to come back. They would lock her up in a hospital room somewhere forever and she would never even see the sun again.

But she couldn't keep lying to Adrianna. It wasn't fair.

"Everything in there is true," Alice said, handing the book over to Adrianna. Adrianna went to take it, but Alice pulled it back. "You have to promise you won't tell anyone. Not even your brothers."

Adrianna nodded. "I promise."

Alice handed her the book. With a heavy sigh, Alice felt the weight of her dread fall over her shoulders. She enjoyed the freedom while she had it, at least.

"I'm really tired," Alice said. She went back into bed and curled up under the covers, her eyes open and staring at the wall.

Adrianna kept her light on. Alice tried not to think about her reading the book. She forced her mind onto something else.

The Cheshire Cat. It was the only other place her mind would go. For all she knew, Cat had been doing this a lot and she had only just found out about it tonight. He might have been back every night since she moved it, looking for it. He might have been watching her all this time, waiting for her to read it.

Something needed to be done about the book. It drove people from Wonderland crazy. She would need to find a way to get rid of it before someone else got to it while she wasn't looking.

And she would need to do it before she was sent to a cozy hospital room for the rest of her life.

CHAPTER 13

A Time to Read

THE NEXT MORNING, Alice woke up unsure if she'd even slept at all. She was exhausted as she rolled over, looking out to the rest of the room where the sunlight was starting to leak through the windows. She had only barely slept.

There was a study block first thing. She could go back to sleep.

She looked across the room to Adrianna, sleeping on top of her covers with her feet on her pillow. The light from her desk was pointed over at the foot of her bed. In her hands, Alice's book had shut itself at some point in the night.

Alice dressed and was about to leave when she looked back at the book in Adrianna's hands. She could take it and try to convince her that it was all in her head. She'd talked to enough doctors who'd taught her just how to do it.

After a moment of standing at the door, she walked back to Adrianna and pulled a sheet of paper off of her desk.

Gone for a walk, she wrote. *See you in class.*

She escaped the dorms without having to talk to anyone. No one was even awake yet, it seemed, so she was free to wander off into the campus. She opted for the front of the grounds with the gardens this time. Those were usually devoid of other students so she could be alone with her thoughts.

She wasn't even sure where to start. She let Adrianna read her notebook that would send her back to the doctors again. Cat was trying to find the book that had driven the Queen of Hearts even more mad. She saw Wonderland everywhere she looked and the more stressed she was, the louder she could hear the beating hearts in her head. Now they were pounding against her skull and no amount of fresh air was going to make it go away.

The gardens weren't even that nice right now. They were withering in the late November cold and many of the bushes were getting bare as the leaves fell off the branches. She should be inside.

Alice looked around to make sure no one was there and let herself think of the window sill overlooking the rooftop garden. She pictured herself sitting there, staring out into the garden, filled with plants that were fighting to remain alive despite the weather.

She sat down and opened her eyes, finding herself already there. That answered whether the treacle was still playing with her.

She brought her knees up to her chest and tried to figure out which of the thoughts was the most pressing.

Adrianna might not even believe anything in the book and she could at least try to convince her that the book was all a story. Cat appearing in the room might have been a nightmare. Alice remembered the doctors convincing her that Wonderland was false. It wouldn't be that hard to do the same thing to Adrianna. And if it didn't work, she wouldn't be sent back to the doctors until after the end of the semester in a few weeks.

And now that she was part treacle, she might be able to run away. Maybe she could live with Lori in England until she came home.

Wonderland was happening somewhere else. Though she kept seeing it everywhere, she wasn't able to go back. Though it continued to haunt her, there was nothing left for her to do about it. She knew the treacle wouldn't bring her back there, or else she would have gone with the amount of time she'd spent thinking about it the past couple weeks.

That left her with Cat. Cat and what he wanted of her.

"I need to get rid of that book," Alice said, suddenly sure of what she was supposed to do.

"You could also read it," a voice said from directly behind her.

Alice jumped and snapped around, finding Cat was sitting in the air over her shoulder, his purple tail flicking impatiently back and forth. The surprise changed quickly into panic that she covered with annoyance. "What are you doing here?" she asked, looking around for anyone else.

"Why Alice," he said, his voice smooth and he moved around to her other side. "What could keep me away?"

"A mouse," she told him flatly. "Leave me alone."

"Now that's not very polite," Cat said, slinking around to the other side, smiling widely.

"Neither is this," she said, thinking about her dorm. She pictured herself sitting on her bed, the blankets still a mess from when she left and the book he wanted her to read still sitting comfortably between the mattresses and out of everyone's reach.

The day had broken fully and the sun was filtering through the cloud cover into the room. She could hear everyone else waking up and in the usual early morning scramble, muffled slightly by the door. Adrianna was no longer in her bed but looking through her wardrobe for a clean sweater.

Adrianna pulled the sweater over her head and looked back to the room, stopping when she saw Alice. "You're back," she said, surprised. "I didn't hear... did you use the door?"

"Um…"

Adrianna's eyes trailed down to Alice's feet. She was wearing shoes in bed after she'd been walking through the garden.

"I can explain," Alice started, though she had no idea where she'd even start.

"Oh, do explain," Cat said, now a boy once more and crawling out from under Adrianna's bed. He rested on his stomach, chin resting in both his hands as he looked up at Alice. "I would love to hear this."

Adrianna jumped and clamped her hands over her mouth, eyes wide and staring down at Cat.

Alice looked frantically from Cat to Adrianna, then back to Cat again. "What do you want?" she demanded at last.

"Want is such a peculiar—"

"Why are you in here?" Alice said quickly, trying to keep his ramblings to a minimum. "You've done enough already. And we both already know what happens when someone reads the book. Why would I want to do that?"

"Well, you know what they say about curiosity," he said, pulling himself out from under the bed and sliding next to Alice in one long movement. He drew a hand under her chin and tilted her face up so her eyes met his. "I also had to see if this rumour about dear little Alice seeing someone was true."

Alice had the sudden desire to smack him hard over the head with the book. She pulled away from him and got off the bed. "I believe they said curiosity killed the cat," Alice said to him, her voice clearly a warning to keep him from continuing. "If you keep talking, that might happen. Leave."

Cat seemed more amused than anything else, making himself comfortable on the bed and facing Alice. "Or you could read the book. I would like to see what in there drove the Queen to finally snap."

"Curiosity kills cats," Alice reminded him again.

"Are you upset because the other children think that you're courting a cat?" he asked, his grin growing even wider. "Or perhaps you are upset because you would like it to happen and you know it never will. If you were to be courting an animal, I dare say I would be quite the catch. Though I am much nicer when I'm in my fur, you know. This body just doesn't suit me, but it does the job for now."

"You're real too?" Adrianna asked, her voice returning though it was quiet. She brought her hands off her face, but kept her eyes fixated on Cat. Alice could see her trying to put together what she was seeing and make sense of it.

Cat's grin grew very wide as he noticed her for the first time. His smile looked like it might even extend past the edges of his face. He shifted and turned in the bed to look right at her, amused and playful. "Although, if I were to choose, I would much rather have this one courting me. I daresay she is much nicer to look at than you are."

"Then annoy her," Alice snapped at him. "And do it somewhere else. I told you to go away."

"You're really the Cheshire Cat?" Adrianna asked, staring at him.

The realization that Adrianna understood what was happening, at least a little, hit her hard. She knew it was the Cheshire Cat in their room and she knew who he was. It looked like she was even starting to believe that this was really happening. If this continued much longer, Alice might have a roommate when they locked her up.

Cat looked Adrianna up and down, shuffling on the bed and drawing closer to her. Alice stepped forward and he shot a glare at her but stopped advancing. He went back to looking over Adrianna, who continued to stand and look on in awe that any of this was happening.

"Interesting company you keep, Alice," he said.

"You need to leave."

"And she is much more polite. She knows better than to be so rude to a guest. I should think she would be more pleasant to deal with. What did you call her?"

Alice's mind raced through her options. She could call for Miss Amanda. She might come running and get rid of Cat, but Adrianna might tell her what happened. Alice had no explanation for this yet, but she couldn't let anyone know that Cat was here. Either they'd be in trouble for being caught with a boy in their dorm or he would leave and Adrianna would tell Miss Amanda exactly what happened, which would be worse. There had to be something else she could do.

She did the first thing she could think of. She brought the water gun to mind again and reached behind her. She closed her hand around it and pulled it back out and fired it at Cat. "Go away!"

Nothing came out. Cat was amused and leaned back against the wall. "I don't think I will," he said. "Although there is one thing you might do to persuade me to leave your lovely abode."

Alice watched, the water gun following as Cat reached his hand up like he was about to grab something. He stopped, puzzled, before glaring at her. "Where is it?" he demanded, turning back to the wall. He reached between the wall and the bed and Alice's heart tightened in her chest. He knew where the book was.

"If it is not anywhere else then it must be here," he reasoned. He pulled the mattress up, knocking the sheets to the ground, but found nothing under there. "You are not clever enough to have hidden it away that well. Where is it? *Where is it?*"

It wasn't there?

He wheeled around and turned on Alice, appearing inches

away from her face. His hands grabbed her shoulders and pulled her in so close that she feared that he might bite her nose off. She could see that he was fuming, the rage in his eyes penetrating through her. She fought to keep eye contact with him and stare right back.

"Leave."

"I will find it," he said, his voice menacing. He vanished slowly, bit by bit until only his eyes remained. "And you will read it. Mark my words, dear, you will read it for me."

And then he was gone.

Alice stayed on her feet for only a moment before sinking to the ground. She dropped the water gun and realized her hands were shaking. All of her was shaking. She brought her knees up to her chest and wrapped her arms around her knees, trying to take deep breaths. He was gone. At least he was gone.

"Alice?"

Alice kept looking straight ahead, though nothing she saw registered. All she could see were his eyes. Beating hearts rang in her ears and she didn't know if it was her own anymore. He'd come back for her and the book. And she didn't even know where the book was anymore.

"It's okay," Adrianna said, dropping down to wrap her arms around Alice. "He's gone now."

She turned to Adrianna and dove to hug her back. She

wasn't sure when the tears started, but they wouldn't stop now, and Adrianna sat there on the floor with her and let her cry.

Alice didn't know how long they stayed like that, but when she finally pulled away and wiped her tears she felt better. "Thanks," she said.

"I don't know why Sarah thinks he likes you," Adrianna said. "He's a jerk."

Alice laughed at that. "He's always been a jerk." She relaxed for a moment before something struck her.

She got up in a panic and went to her mattress, now knocked askew. "Where is it?" she asked, reaching under the mattresses and trying to feel under the bed in case it had slipped down there.

"Oh," Adrianna said, going back to her own bed. She pulled out an old, leather bound brown book from under her pillow. "You mean this?"

Alice looked back and saw it and the monster on the cover in Adrianna's hand. She froze, staring at it.

"I finished your book and I wanted to see if it was true and I saw you checking for something behind your bed and Mike and Mark and Matt all hide things between their mattresses when they don't want anyone finding them and I checked and I found the book and I was curious so I looked in it and I was going to return it tonight, but—"

"You took it?" Alice asked. "And you believe me?"

"I…"

Alice hugged her, a wave of relief washing over her. "Thank you," she said, pulling away and taking a deep breath. "But look, you can't tell anyone anything, okay? You don't want them to send you to the doctors. Trust me."

"I promise I won't tell anyone," Adrianna said, a smile growing on her face and giving her back the book. "You can tell me anything and I won't tell anyone. But what do we do about the book?"

Alice looked down to the monster on the cover. Her fear of it had waned since keeping it between the mattresses. She didn't know how to let the creature out and it had stayed locked inside the pages. Without whatever the Queen of Hearts had said, it seemed that this was nothing more than a regular book so long as she never read it.

"You could just read it," Adrianna suggested. "He said he'd go away if you did."

"No! No, it drives people mad. Well, mad*der*. The Queen of Hearts is mad with power and look at what happened to Cat. He wasn't like this before the book."

Alice took a deep breath. "I have to hide it," she said, immediately thinking of the perfect place. "I'll see you in class."

With that, Alice vanished.

CHAPTER 14

Boy Trouble

"HE'S LOOKING AT you again," Sarah said as they headed back to the dorms.

Alice nodded but didn't look up from her book of poetry, trying to pick out the rhyme scheme of each of the poems.

"Alice, he's looking."

"Okay."

"He likes you."

"Okay."

"God, Alice, are you even listening to me?"

"Okay."

"Alice!" Sarah turned on her and stopped right in front of her.

Alice looked up from her book. "What?"

"Cat's totally got a thing for you."

"Oh," Alice said, turning back to her book and walking around Sarah.

"What is wrong with you? He's hot!"

"He's a jerk," Adrianna said, stepping between the two of them. "Alice can do a lot better."

Alice came to appreciate Adrianna more since telling her. With Cat seeming to follow Alice around the school, showing up just to watch where she was going, Sarah had gotten it in her head that he had a crush. Adrianna had started distracting Sarah when she started trying to get anything out of Alice about it.

"So?" Sarah asked. "He's hot. And he might be waiting to ask her to the dance."

Alice hurried ahead and was glad to find Kevin and Robert already at the table. "Alice!" Robert said, trying and failing to keep his voice down. "You gotta help me. I don't get any of this Egypt stuff."

She set her bag down and went to Robert's side to start helping him through the mythology when Sarah and Adrianna joined them. Sarah seemed to have dropped the subject now, opening their books and getting started on studying for the next set of exams tomorrow.

It lasted for all of half an hour before Heather joined them.

"Where have you been?" Sarah asked, immediately abandoning her English notes as Heather sat down.

"I had to do some stuff," Heather said, though she met no one's eyes. Though she tried to hide it, Alice saw a faint blush.

"Someone asked you out!" Sarah said.

"It's none of your business." Heather refused to look up from her bag.

"But who—"

"Can we just study?"

Sarah turned back to her homework, but her eyes stayed on Heather, studying her closely. Heather ignored her as she sat down at the opposite end of the table. She kept her eyes down and her shoulders up.

After a few moments of silence and staring between the two, Alice's eyes met Adrianna's for a moment. She looked more concerned than confused, but Alice didn't want to ask why. Instead, she looked down at Adrianna's empty worksheet.

"Need a hand?" Alice asked quietly. Adrianna nodded and they started working on figuring out what a quatrain was. Though Adrianna had memorized the definition, she could not find one in the poems without someone spelling it out for her.

The tension started to disperse and the studying got back on track. She and Adrianna worked on the poetry revision and

Kevin was there soon to try and figure out what the meanings were behind the poems so they would know what to write for their essays.

Robert was fidgeting in his seat, still struggling to memorize the Egyptian Gods and what they all stood for. His eyes kept flickering around the table before looking down at his work again. He tapped the pencil on the table, but did not write anything. Finally, he smacked it down on the table.

"You okay, dude?" Kevin asked.

"Does everyone have a date?"

"One person might have a date," Kevin said quickly.

"But—"

"I don't have a date. Sarah, you going with anyone?"

Sarah hesitated.

"Adrianna? Alice?"

"We know Cat is going to ask Alice," Sarah said.

Alice got up and grabbed her books. "I have to go," she said, not looking at any of them as she turned and left.

"Alice," Kevin called after her, but she didn't stop.

She didn't slow down until she felt the biting chill of early December's freezing cold air. Once she was outside, she got out of the way of the door and shoved her books back in her bag, taking a slow and steadying breath. It wasn't anger that welled up inside her so much as a deep desire for Sarah to stop talking about Cat. She didn't know what she was talking about and no matter how many times Alice told her that it wasn't true, she wouldn't listen. Instead she would demand to know details about how she'd known him in the past.

She needed to come up with that story at some point. After finals.

"Alice!"

She turned around to find both Heather and Adrianna had followed her out. Heather reached her first, worried.

"You okay?"

"I'm fine," Alice said. "I just needed some air."

"Don't worry about Sarah," Heather said, draping an arm around Alice. "She's just being... Sarah. She's obsessed with the match making stuff. Can't seem to get a date for herself, though."

Heather laughed at this and Alice offered an uncomfortable smile. That seemed to be enough for Heather, who let Alice go and shot a quick glance at Adrianna before leaning in again. "And just between the two of us, I got a date two weeks ago."

She leaned back and smiled. "If you don't want to come back in, that's fine. I'll see you after the test tomorrow?"

"Yeah," Alice said, not really sure what was happening. She waved Heather off and picked her backpack up again.

Adrianna watched her go before turning back to Alice. "You're okay?"

"I'm fine," Alice said. "Really. You can go back."

"I think I need a break."

Alice smiled and couldn't think of anything else to say to that, instead starting to walk. Adrianna fell in step next to her and followed Alice's lead as she started to wander through the campus. Only a few people were wandering around and even those people looked nervous or had a book in their hands. Even the sky seemed nervous, the clouds high above them stirring.

She let her mind wander. She'd let the stress of finals overwhelm the stress of Cat following her and trying to find the book. She hid it away and had neither told Adrianna where it was or even checked to see if it was still there. As far as she was concerned, if Cat was still following her instead of talking to her, he hadn't found it yet.

She saw something moving out of the corner of her eye and looked back. Two of Adrianna's brothers were heading into the school behind them. From this angle, it looked like they were going into the windows, which reflected not the grounds, but the grounds of the castle, now with the garden overgrown and the Red Knight patrolling through it.

She tore her eyes away and back out to the school grounds. The Red Knight was nowhere to be found and the lawns looked as desolate as they had a moment ago. She tried to force those thoughts out of her mind and tried to think of nothing at all for at least a moment. It all felt like too much was happening.

"I wanted to ask you something," Adrianna said a few feet later, stopping Alice in front of the window of the school and looking at it. "Is that Wonderland? The castle, I mean. Not the window."

Alice looked at it, still seeing the castle's grounds with the Red Knight patrolling it. She looked back at Adrianna, studying her face. "How long have you been seeing it?" she asked, her voice quiet.

"Since you fell in the pond," Adrianna said. "I think other people have been seeing it too, but I've been seeing it a lot lately."

"Other people?" Alice took a reflexive step backwards, scared at the thought. Other people had seen Wonderland? Or it could be something worse.

She looked around, scanning the school and the grounds for any sign of something purple. "It's probably Cat," she said, not sure if she should be more or less worried. "He was able to send me into Wonderland. He can probably do that too."

"I can do a great many things," a voice purred from the air behind her. "Though I will be happy to claim credit for this as well, and I will do so myself. I do not need others claiming it for me."

Adrianna let out a small yelp of surprise and covered her mouth.

"Cat." Alice snapped around to see as only his head upside down hung before her, his grin not so wide, though his teeth looking quite a bit sharper than she remembered. "You found it."

"I shall claim that when it happens as well," he said. He was slowly appearing, turning over as more of his body appeared until he was once more towering over Alice. "You've become a clever girl. Perhaps too clever."

He was making too much sense. Alice didn't trust it. She kept herself between Cat and Adrianna. Bringing the water gun to mind again, this time specifically thinking of a loaded one, she reached behind her and grabbed one, keeping it firmly in hand.

"You seem frightened," Cat said, sliding closer until his face was right in front of Alice's, his sharp teeth on full display as he smiled. "Why would you be frightened of a cat, I wonder? Especially one with such a simple request."

"I won't read the book for you," Alice said firmly.

"You will!" he demanded, grabbing her by the shoulders and leaning down over her.

Alice froze as he did so, panic coursing through her. She hesitated before bringing the gun out from behind her back and shot Cat with it, the water spraying under his chin. He let go and she kept shooting him in the face.

Cat slipped away and vanished. Alice kept the gun pointed at the air where he had been as she looked around for where he disappeared to.

Adrianna yelped again and Alice spun around. Cat had Adrianna by the shoulders with his fingers snaking around her neck, holding her up against the window.

"You will find it and you will read it. I must know what drove the Queen mad."

"Let her go," Alice demanded, swinging the water gun back at him. "Adrianna has nothing to do with this."

"Ah," he said, grinning at the gun. "You wouldn't want me to drop this into Wonderland. How do you think she might fare? I hear the Queen of Hearts is looking for a pretty daughter. Perhaps she might even let her keep her heart."

Adrianna struggled in his grip, her hands pulling on his and her legs not quite hitting when she tried kicking. Her sounds of struggle were quiet and her face was going red from the effort. Her back didn't compress against the glass of the window, but seemed to go right through Wonderland where the Red Knight might see her hanging in the garden.

Alice dropped the water gun, letting it clatter to the ground.

Cat grinned a little wider but did not let Adrianna go.

"There's a small task left for you yet," he said. "You have been so busy reading so many other books. One more will not harm you. Unless you wish your curious friend here to see just what that book has wrought in Wonderland for herself."

"Hey!" Alice heard someone yell. She looked at the window, but the Red Knight had moved on. "Let her go!"

Someone with light brown hair and a high school uniform rushed past her and grabbed Cat, pulling him off Adrianna and slamming him against the brick beside the window. Alice rushed forward to pull Adrianna away from the window and she fell forward onto the path.

Alice looked up, Travis holding Cat off the ground and pinning him to the building. "Hands off my sister."

More people descended on them, though Alice barely noticed two of the triplets helping her and Adrianna to their feet. Joe asked them what happened and if they were all right, but Alice wasn't listening. She rose with them, her attention still on Cat.

Cat didn't take his eyes off of her. He stared at her, his grin shrinking into something much more menacing. He shrugged and twisted, easily slipping out of Travis' grasp and slunk around him and down the path.

Travis looked at his hands, trying to figure out how he got out of his grip. Joe tried to grab after him, but Cat was too quick.

Cat turned back where the building ended. "It will happen," he said. His eyes stayed on Alice as he slunk around the corner of the building.

Travis rushed after him, but Joe grabbed him by the arm. "What happened?" he asked.

Adrianna looked to Alice.

"I don't know," Alice said, trying desperately to come up with something, but she couldn't even think. "He just…"

"He tried to ask Alice to the dance," Adrianna said. "He got mad when she said no."

Joe looked between both of them. Alice could tell he didn't believe them, but he seemed to accept it anyway. "You two should get back to your dorm. We'll track down Evan and see about what we can do about Cat. And you two."

Mike and Matt rolled their eyes. "Yeah we know," Mike said. "No more trying to sabotage exams we don't want to take."

"We'll walk you back," Matt said, ushering them both onward down the path and back to the dorms.

Alice stooped down and picked up the water gun she dropped before falling in step with the two of them. She looked to Adrianna, whose eyes were on her as they walked. Glancing first at her brothers, she whispered, "Thank you."

Adrianna smiled, but stayed quiet as her brothers turned back to look at them.

"Looks like turning him down was a bad idea," Matt said.

"Or a really good one," Mike countered. "Addie, you sure you're okay?"

"Yeah, I'm fine," she said.

Mike wasn't paying attention to her anymore, reaching to take the gun from Alice's hand. Alice let him remove it and he studied the orange and blue water gun as they walked. "Where did you get this?"

"Found it," Alice said. "Why?"

He pointed to a small etching on the bottom of the handle with the initials LMC. "This is mine."

"Oh." Alice said nothing else.

CHAPTER 15

First Dance

FINALS PASSED WITHOUT Alice even seeing Cat again. Instead, Alice was almost certain that she and Adrianna had a shadow in the form of her brothers. She kept seeing them wherever they went. It was comforting and Alice started to relax again, feeling that Cat wouldn't come back while there were people around, much less ones who might throw a punch.

Even better were the mirrors. Alice rarely saw Wonderland anymore now that she wasn't so stressed out about finals or Cat suddenly appearing to threaten her again. It left her with only a few things to think about, though there was only one thing anyone wanted to talk about in the dorms now that finals were over.

When the day of the dance came, they were getting ready in Heather and Sarah's room on Sarah's insistence. Alice thought it was because it gave Sarah a chance to show off how grown up she was, or maybe just her makeup collection that spanned her desk when laid out. Still, she was a lot nicer after Robert asked her to the dance. At the very least, she stopped mentioning Cat and her thoughts about how she thought he felt about Alice whenever the opportunity arose.

Neither Adrianna nor Alice had dates. For Adrianna, she knew that had something to do with their shadows keeping all of the boys away from their sister. For her part, she didn't mind. She didn't know how to dance and intended on hanging out on the side with her friends when they weren't dancing anyway.

Getting ready for the dance, though, was a little more involved than just brushing her hair and putting on a dress.

"What is this?" Adrianna asked, holding the tube of something in her fingers like it might explode at any moment.

Sarah turned back to see what Adrianna had. "Eyeliner," Sarah said. "Alice, can you help her?"

Alice pulled the tube out of Adrianna's hands and put it back down on the table. She picked up the black one instead and turned to Adrianna as she opened it. "Look up."

"Where did you learn to do this?" Adrianna asked, straining to keep her eyes open.

"My sister," Alice said. "Stop blinking so much." Alice did Adrianna's makeup and touched up her own.

"I still can't believe no one asked you guys," Heather said once Sarah was done with her hair.

Once she was satisfied with Adrianna's eyes, Alice handed her a tube of red lip gloss and moved on to doing her own. She didn't get much chance to use makeup at home when Lori wasn't there to show her what to do. It was surprising to her how much she remembered.

"It's not that bad," Adrianna said. "We can still hang out with you guys, right?"

"But isn't it weird? You're really pretty and *no one* asked you?"

Alice stayed perfectly silent as she finished adjusting her appearance in the mirror and kept her knowing smile to herself. With her brothers watching both of them, it would be easy for them to dissuade any of the boys who wanted to ask her to rethink it.

"I can't believe Matt Case asked you and you didn't tell me!" Sarah chimed in, looking between Heather and Adrianna. "Either of you!"

"He didn't tell me!" Adrianna said, laughing.

"Are you guys almost done?" Alice asked, glancing at the time. "You're supposed to meet them downstairs soon."

"How do I look?" Sarah asked, smoothing down her dress and spinning around. The red skirt of her dress flared out and fell back once she came to a halt. The curls on her head did not move, the hairspray locking it firmly in place.

"Great," Alice said. "Both of you," she added, turning to Heather. She was dressed in bright pink and Sarah had wound her thick, black hair up around her head in a braid.

"Thanks," Heather said.

They gathered their things into small purses and headed out. Alice and Adrianna lingered behind, picking up their shoes and coats from their own room. When they came back out, they peered out into the foyer where couples and groups of people were meeting before heading out.

Heather and Sarah were in the crowd, meeting up with their dates for the night. Alice pulled Adrianna back, retying the bow at the back of her shimmering deep blue dress. Adrianna checked Alice's pale blue one, though it was simple enough that it needed no adjusting

When they looked again, both Heather and Sarah were gone. They threw on their coats and made their way through the bustle of people in the foyer to the door. The crowds were thinning out now as dates and groups met one another.

"Would you two lovely ladies like an escort?"

They stopped and turned, Kevin standing behind them in a jacket and offering both of his arms to them. Adrianna took it first and Alice shrugged and followed in suit. They headed out towards the hall.

"Thank you," Adrianna said, giggling.

Alice smiled and said nothing, looking up at the snow gently falling down around them. With the exams and the dance, she'd almost forgotten that this was their last night on campus until the next semester. She was going to head back home soon. Her father would have probably heard that she'd fallen ill and that a boy with purple hair named Cat had been involved. He might have even heard that Cat had been following her.

If he had, then she'd never see the campus again. He may have not, but just in case, she drank in the look of the campus with the snow falling softly over it, coating it in an untouched blanket of white. She made friends. She did well in class. For the first time in years, she was happy.

If it weren't for Cat and Wonderland, she might have been happy here for a long time. Now, she didn't even know if she'd return after the break.

But there was still tonight. She turned back, finding Kevin and Adrianna deep in conversation about the finer details of Robert asking Sarah out. They were laughing. Alice looked back over the grounds as they walked.

Yes, she still had one more night. Cat hadn't even shown his face, either of them, since that day.

"What about you, Alice?"

"What?" she asked, turning back Adrianna and Kevin.

"Did you ever have dances at your old school?" Adrianna asked.

"I was homeschooled," Alice said. Adrianna looked disappointed and Alice opted to change the subject. "So why didn't you ask anyone, Kevin?"

Kevin rolled his eyes and smiled. "Because I have been to a dance before. Last year my school held one for all of the grade sixes and made us go with someone. I got paired with this one girl who I thought would be okay to hang out with, but she wouldn't let me go see my friends all night and kept wanting me to compliment her. It was so annoying."

"You could have found someone. What about Adrianna?"

Adrianna blushed a bright shade of red.

"That wasn't really an option," Kevin said, shifting nervously as they walked.

Alice nodded, but Adrianna looked back up confused. "Why not?"

"Oh look, we're here already," Kevin said, smiling a bit too much as he pointed out the Hall. With the snowfall in the moonlight, it looked like it was sparkling. People were trickling in from all over campus in the snow, dressed in all sorts of colours, meeting people by the doors where there was some cover, or wandering inside. The closer they came, the more Alice could hear and feel the beat of the music resonating from the building.

The first thing Alice noticed once they got inside was just how loud it was. The music blared through the hall, but louder still were the people trying to talk over it. Everyone was dressed in their best, with dress shirts and dresses instead of their uniforms. High school students mingled amidst the middle school students and the teachers stayed to the side, out of the way of those who were already taking the opportunity to hit the dance floor.

"This is amazing," Alice said, looking around and smiling.

They laughed and found a small table near the snacks to sit and chat, watching everyone else start to celebrate the end of the semester. They spotted Heather easily enough, then Sarah and Robert a moment later. Robert looked nervous.

Kevin asked Adrianna to dance soon after, Alice being left to guard the table. It soon filled with purses and people as her friends came and went from the dance floor. She found that she loved watching everyone in their finest having fun and dancing the night away. Even when her friends did come back, she continued to watch.

"You sure you don't want to dance?" Sarah asked with a drink in hand. She and Robert spent so much time on the floor that Alice was surprised that Sarah wasn't completely out of breath.

Alice shook her head. "I don't know how to dance."

"When has that ever stopped anyone?" Mark asked, taking a seat to her right at the table.

"It's okay," Alice said. "I like watching everyone. Maybe I'll dance at the next one. Sarah can teach me for next time."

If I get to come to another one. A pang of regret hit her that she wasn't giving it a shot, but she would rather remember the night fondly than embarrassing herself by trying to do something she had no idea how to do.

"A pretty girl like you shouldn't just be a wallflower all night," he said.

Alice blushed and looked down. "Thanks," she muttered, though she wasn't really sure why she suddenly felt so embarrassed. He was just being nice. She looked much more plain than most of the girls there. "I'll be okay."

"I think you'll do fine," Mark said, taking her by the hand and pulling her out to the floor. "Let's visit Addie. She's barely had a chance to sit yet, has she?" Alice tried to protest, looking back to Sarah when words failed her. She waved Alice off and smirked as Alice was swallowed up by the dance floor.

Once Mark found a spot, he spun her and started to guide her through something that was definitely not the small back and forth stepping everyone else was doing. He went slowly until she managed to find the beat, watching his feet and mimicking them until she was comfortable with it. Once she was, he started moving her closer and farther and in circles.

Alice just tried to follow along clumsily, though she was starting to get it.

When the music started to slow, he spun her once more and she was somewhere else with a different dance partner. She laughed, a small nervous laugh as she waited for her head to stop spinning in the arms of her new partner. He moved them in slow circles, also in something that felt much different than anything she'd seen anyone else doing tonight.

"You really do look quite lovely tonight."

Alice snapped her head up to see who the velvet voice dancing with her was. Cat stood there, holding her in a waltz and guiding them both to the edge of the Hall. She tried to pull away, but he was holding her too tightly for her to break free.

"What are you doing here?" she demanded. Her mind was racing through the options. Her right hand was detained. She might still be able to pull something out with her left, but someone might see it. She stopped moving with him, but he pulled her along anyway and she felt her feet lift off the ground as he made a large, sweeping turn.

Cat grinned his usual wide grin, though he seemed a little more crazed than before. "I think we've played this game long enough, dear. It is time to concede your defeat."

Alice kept looking around, trying to find some opening. She could run for it, but she couldn't see a door anywhere near her. She could pull the water gun out from behind *his* back, though when she looked to her hand, it was trembling.

"Are you afraid of me?" he asked, amused. "It's almost as if you expect me to have stolen something from you. Something you have kept so carefully hidden."

"You found the book?"

"It's simple enough to satisfy me enough to make me leave. Just read the book. Once you do that, I'll be happy and I'll go. Is that really so hard?"

The dance left her mind as panic rushed through her.

No. He couldn't have.

Alice pulled away and vanished from the dance floor.

CHAPTER 16

Jabberwocky

SHE THOUGHT SHE went deaf. The silence didn't sound right, like she was listening to it through cotton with the faint memory of a beat still pounding in her ears. Even her eyes took a moment to adjust from the faint fluorescent lighting to the soft moonlight streaming in through the window through the gently falling snow.

At least it still smelled like the library. She breathed in the scent of musty, untouched books and forced herself to remain still while her eyes adjusted to the light.

Her vision came back too slowly. As soon as she could make out the shelf in front of her, she started feeling along the spines for the brown leather one she'd hidden here. It was a spot near the back, a place that you needed special permission to access. She wasn't sure what it was about these books that were so special, but most of the books here had a light layer of dust over them. Very few people came here. It was the perfect spot.

There was no gap in the shelf where a book might have been removed, but three of them that felt like they might be the one. She raced her fingers back over the spines and pulled out the one that made her feel the most uneasy.

Her eyes were adjusted enough to see the beast on the cover. He hadn't found it.

"Ah, clever girl," came the Cat's voice came from behind her. She felt his fur press into her neck and his claws sank into her shoulder. "Keep the book with plenty of its kind. Nice of you to ensure it is not lonely."

Alice wrenched her shoulder free from his claws and turned on him. "You lied! You said you found it!"

His tail twitched. "I do not lie, dear. Now come, let's see this book that has caused so much trouble."

Alice pulled the book closer to her chest and closed her eyes as she backed away from him.

The back of her leg collided with something and she fell onto her bed. Alice let go of the breath she didn't realize she was holding and forced herself to take a few deep breaths before getting back to her feet and looking around the room.

She had to hide the book before he found her again. She wouldn't read it, but he couldn't read it either. Not when he was also here. People here couldn't have their hearts ripped out and survive like they could in Wonderland.

She pushed the thought out of her mind and looked back to her bed. Back under the mattress. He knew the spot, but maybe he wouldn't think she would hide it there again.

Purple eyes appeared hovering over her bed, followed by a wide grin. He'd already found her.

Clutching the book close, she closed her eyes and went to the first place she thought of.

The cold barely registered with the adrenaline pumping through her veins. She was standing under Cat's tree, still wearing only a dress and shoes that were not suitable for the snow. She looked to the pond, thinking maybe she could throw the book in there, but her eye caught something else first.

His purple hair shimmered in the moonlight. Cat lay along the low branch of the tree, once again a boy rather than a cat, watching her intently. He looked like he had gone from mad to deranged, though when he spoke his voice was low.

"I think this game is done, little mouse," he said, his voice smooth and his eyes leering at the book in her hands. "I'll find you wherever you go. It really is best that you just read it and satisfy my curiosity."

Alice's heart dropped and she thought about running

again, but she felt his grip tighten on her shoulder. She wasn't going to be able to outrun him forever.

Desperate, she raised the book over her head and flung it out into the middle of the pond. It did not sink or even break the surface of the ice, instead landing with a clunk and skittering away.

Cat dove out from the tree, tackling Alice down onto the ice. She felt it crack a little under her. He pressed her shoulders into the frozen surface of the pond. He sat on her and pinned her down, one hand holding her head onto the ice. With his other, he reached and brought the book back from the other shore and propped it up on the ice in front of Alice's face. He turned the book sideways for her and opened it to the first page.

"Read."

She struggled against his grasp, trying to wriggle free, but he had her pinned down. She couldn't even think of anywhere she would run to, since she knew he would only continue to follow her everywhere. And now he had the book.

"I won't," she said. She tried to look up at him, but he kept her head down, her ear pressed against the ice, the cold radiating painfully up into her eardrum. There was only the book in front of her and the strange writing inside.

"I think you will. Unless you'd like to remain here.

You're already so cold, dear. One little task and you can go back inside."

He was right. She was already starting to lose the feeling in her hands and feet. The more she struggled, the more she could feel the ice start to crack beneath her.

She looked at the book and the writing on the pages. There were letters there, but they all looked wrong, like they had been written backwards. "I can't read it," Alice said.

"You've been a studious girl all semester," Cat said. "You can read well and good."

"It's not written normally. It's backwards."

"Excuses!" he said, a laugh in his voice as he slammed Alice's head against the ice. She heard a crack beneath her. "You will read this book for me, dear, if it takes us all night."

Alice's head was spinning and her eyes couldn't find the page. The words floated around her, moving in lazy circles until they finally settled down on the ice.

There was no point in running anymore. Maybe she was worried over nothing. Maybe it just wouldn't work for her. She wasn't from Wonderland, after all. She wasn't mad like them. She might not go mad at all. The creature in the book might not listen to her.

Or maybe the creature would appear and rip out Cat's heart. It might throw him back in Wonderland where she wouldn't have to deal with him anymore.

"Read," Cat hissed.

She blinked, looking at the reflection of the words in the ice and took a deep breath. Carefully, she recited the strange poem, filled with words she did not recognize and the names of beasts she hadn't read about in her books. She didn't know what a Jubjub bird was and she didn't care what a vorpal blade could do. The Bandersnatch and Jabberwock mentioned, the Tumtum tree, at this moment, she did not care. Word by word, she read it until she finished the entire thing.

Alice felt strange as she finished the poem. She felt a little strange the whole time she was reading it, like something was helping her along to pronounce the words that she didn't recognize, but even stranger when she finished.

Cat was grinning ear to ear when he bent down to turn the page. "Now that wasn't so terribly difficult." he said. "Only a few hundred more pages to go."

Alice looked past him and at the book. A slender porcelain claw was creeping out from the cover.

Cat followed her gaze to the book and the claw coming out of it. He tossed the book to the snow on the other side of the pond and skittered off Alice away from it. Alice backed up to the edge of the pond away from him, but Cat kept his eyes on the book and the creature coming out of it.

Carefully, Cat crept closer to the book as more long fingers started to come out of it. The claws came first, but the rest of the finger started to creep out as well. Cat kept drawing nearer to it like he was about to touch it, then backing away as the thing inside the book twitched.

Alice pinched the inside of her wrist.

No. This was something that happened in Wonderland, not here.

Something underneath her lurched and she felt herself start to fall. She grabbed the edge of the pond and scrambled up onto the shore, looking back to see what was happening.

The pond was no longer a pond, but a window down into a bright day. The sun shone down on a small cottage that Alice remembered belonged to the White Rabbit. Outside there were now several small statues of creatures that appeared to be made of metal.

The image was rippling out from where she was. When it reached far enough that it was under Cat, he stumbled. Uncertain of his footing, he looked down and immediately tried to scramble away from the ice and disappear, but he wasn't fast enough. He fell through, Alice watching as he changed back to a Cat as he dropped back into Wonderland.

A large foot reached out of the book, black as ink and looking like it was made of shadows. It stomped hard against the ground, making the earth shake and Alice grabbed onto the grass under the snow so that she wouldn't fall back into Wonderland herself.

She watched as the shadows started to pour out of the book and scatter in a mess of dark shapes dancing in the moonlight. They swirled up high into the sky and started to swoop down. Alice covered her head with her bare arms and pressed herself into the snow, curling up small and hoping the large black mass above her didn't notice. She felt the wind pick up as it grew larger and peered through the gap in her arms as it swirled and came together into something large.

It turned towards her and she saw four white eyes look at her. She felt like she was being marked by the creature, though she couldn't tell if it was trying to say thank you or marking her as prey for the future. She couldn't keep her eyes off of it, even as it turned away and raced into the forest, shadows continuing to follow along behind it.

It only lasted a moment, but it left her heart racing. She was shaking and tried to take a few deep breaths to calm herself back down. She pushed herself up off the grass, brushing the snow off her dress and realizing just how numb her hands and feet were. Still, she made herself walk to the book and pick it up. Cat was gone, but it was still too dangerous to leave alone.

It was over now and she needed to get herself together. She was at the dance. She'd been at the dance with her friends for the last night at Lucena Academy. She was dancing and now she knew that was a bad idea for the future. When she was there, someone cut in and she eventually got lost and just stepped out for some air. Yes, that should be good enough.

When she looked back at the pond, it was once more covered in an ordinary sheet of ice.

With the book in hand, she held it close and looked down over herself. She was sure her makeup was running and her hair was out of place. She didn't have much of an explanation for that or why her dress was so wet, but hopefully everyone would be so busy with the dance that they wouldn't notice that she looked like she'd been in a fight. They might also not notice that she was now holding a large book. Even with the low light, the book would be difficult to explain.

Curious, she opened it again. Her hands were still shaking and every move she tried to make with them hurt, but she still managed to get the book open. The first page was empty.

"You saw that, right? It was over here."

"We don't have time for this if we're going to—"

"Hey, isn't that..."

Alice took a deep breath as she saw two of Adrianna's brothers draw nearer. She slipped the book behind her back and tried to make it and her hand move back into her dorm room. Her hand went, but the book just dropped onto the snow behind her. She snapped her hand back and spun around, picking up the book and turning back to see both Mark and Mike were standing in front of her, arms crossed and studying her.

"You," Mark said.

Alice smiled. "Hello," she said, relaxing her shoulders and ready with her story.

"You disappeared."

"Someone cut in," Alice said.

"You're not at the dance anymore."

"I just needed a little air."

"The dance is about ten minutes across campus."

"A lot of air," she said quickly. "I'm surprised to see you two out here."

"We were just taking a walk."

"Ten minutes across campus?"

Mark looked her over a moment, trying to think of some way to respond.

Mike offered her his coat. "You don't ask, we don't ask."

Alice smiled and took the coat, still warm from being around him. She rubbed at her arms and hands, trying to get the feeling properly back into them. "Deal."

They walked back to the dance, saying nothing as Alice tried to warm herself up. Alice didn't quite know what to say, carefully avoiding both of their eyes when they looked like they were about to ask what happened to her. She'd make them tell her what they were doing first if she had to.

Once they drew near and the brothers pulled her back behind the next building. She looked around the corner and saw why. There were several chaperones patrolling the outside of the dance, stopping students when they tried to leave and keeping an eye on those who felt the need to take a break outside.

"How are you at climbing?" Mark asked her.

Alice looked between him and Mike, confused. She looked back and up, seeing that there was a spot up between the roof of this building and the hall where the dance was being held that didn't look too wide.

"I have my own way back in," Alice told them. "Can you do me a favour?"

"Why should we—"

"Yes," Mike said, elbowing his brother hard. "What is it?"

"Tell Adrianna to meet me in the bathroom with my purse?"

"Fine," Mark said. "See you back inside."

Alice watched as the two of them scaled up the side of the building using the lattice, neither having a problem with the snow or the cold as they climbed.

Once they were out of sight, she closed her eyes and went back to her dorm room, slipping the book under her pillow.

And then she was in the foyer of the hall. Quickly, she found the bathroom and went to the mirror. Running makeup was the least of her worries. Her hair stuck out at strange angles underneath her hair band and a red welt was already forming on her temple. She took off Mike's coat and started trying to brush her hair down with her fingers, but they were still shaking.

She stared down at her hands and tried to make them stop shaking. They didn't need to be shaking. There was nothing left for her to be scared of.

The beat of the music morphed in her head, sounding again like the beating of hundreds of trapped hearts pulsing against the walls. Cat would be back there now and she almost hoped that his heart would join the rest as compensation for how he'd tormented her. That book had driven him mad as well, and he never even read it.

Alice forced herself to take a deep breath. She needed to pull herself together. She only had one last night with friends before the break and she might never get to see them again. She had read the book and not been driven insane by it. The book might not have any effect on her at all.

She grabbed a paper towel and ran it under water before she used it to wipe the makeup off her face. When she closed her eyes, she could see the strange creature's four eyes staring back at her.

Not tonight. She wouldn't worry about the creature tonight. There were other things to worry about, like the red bump forming on the side of her head where Cat had slammed her head into the ice. It looked like it had bled a little, but it wasn't too bad. It didn't even hurt anymore.

"Oh my god!" Adrianna said, bursting in and taking a look at Alice. "What happened?"

"I had a run in with Cat," Alice said, taking the purse from her hands and starting to fix her makeup. There was nothing she could do about the bruise forming on her head, so instead she took off her hair band and let her hair cover it.

"It's over now," Alice said, replacing her makeup and moving her hair to cover the redness. "Cat's gone back to Wonderland. He's not going to bother anyone anymore."

Alice knew that was a lie.

CHAPTER 17

Hope

ALICE WASN'T SURE how she made it through the night. She'd thrown herself into the dance, accepting the hand of anyone who asked her, which wasn't many people, and trying desperately to keep up with the shuffling everyone else in her year was more comfortable with.

At the end of the night, she'd fallen on her bed without even taking off her shoes. She was asleep before her head hit the pillow.

The morning came too soon. Light streamed in from their window, pestering her eyelids until they finally opened and she let out a groan, rolling back over in bed to shield her eyes. It wasn't the next day yet. She didn't want to face the day yet.

A faint humming permeated her attempts to get back to sleep and she reluctantly sat back up, looking around the room.

Adrianna looked like she had been awake for at least an

hour, humming to herself with headphones on. Her side of the room was covered in school books and clothes. A suitcase was still closed at her feet.

"Already?" Alice asked, wiping a hand over her face. It came back black. Looking down at her pillow, she realized she'd slept in her makeup.

She got out of bed and went to the shower, Adrianna not even turning around as she hummed and sang along to her music.

Once the warm stream of water started pouring over her, Alice made herself relax as her mind went over everything. She was nervous, but not only because she didn't want to go home. It was because she didn't know if she would ever be back again.

She went over the year and tried to count the things that they called her parents about. She'd disappeared for a day and nearly gotten pneumonia thanks to a trip to Wonderland, though they only called that time about her illness and falling in the pond. The administration didn't know she'd been stalked by Cat. Even if they had, he seemed to just be another student to anyone else and nothing unusual. Her grades had been good and she handed in her assignments on time.

It all came down to whether or not Evan had reported Cat attacking Adrianna and if the administration had then called her parents about it. Even if they had, it wasn't her fault. It might not matter, but she clung to that fact.

She ran a hand over the bruise forming on her right temple. At least no one knew what had happened to her last night.

She had to come back to school. Even with Cat back in Wonderland, she'd still released something out of the book into the woods. She knew it was something else she was going to have to deal with. Those eyes, she knew they remembered her and she knew they would find a way to meet again, regardless of whether she made it back.

Alice finally stepped out of the washroom, dressed with a towel around her wet hair. Adrianna was still pulling things out of her closet, singing to some new tune, and Alice didn't interrupt her, instead sitting down at her desk and opening her notebook.

Everything from last night was on her mind. She needed to get it out of there and she couldn't let herself slip up when her father was around. If she managed to keep herself out of trouble with him for this long, she wasn't going to wreck it by letting anything slip when she was already home free.

She started writing everything that happened last night. Pieces of it started to come together as she did. The reason Cat never found the book was because, as far as she could tell, he only ever knew how to find her. He was just following her everywhere she went.

Nothing explained the portal to Wonderland, though. It was lucky, but it didn't make any sense.

When she looked up again, it was an hour later. Adrianna's side of the room had been completely cleaned up and she was just putting the finishing touches on her bed. She glanced over her shoulder and caught Alice watching her.

"Good morning," she said. "I didn't want to interrupt."

"Sorry," Alice said.

"You were writing about last night, right?"

"Yeah." Alice looked at the book, as well as the one still sitting in the corner of her desk, untouched since Adrianna had read it. She would probably be back after the break, but if not she needed to take care of the books.

She picked both of the books and handed them to Adrianna. "Can you hang on to these for me?"

"Why?" Adrianna asked, taking them and holding them like they were about to crumble in her hands. "You could leave them here if you don't want to bring them home."

"I just don't want anyone reading them."

"So why don't you take them home?"

Alice hesitated a moment. "I'd rather you held onto them for me," she said. "My bag is already going to be heavy and you look like you barely put anything in yours."

"I'm coming back," Adrianna said with a bit of a laugh. She put the books in her bag.

Alice got her own suitcase out from the bottom of her wardrobe, already mostly packed. Adrianna put her iPod into her speakers and gave them both a little music to listen to.

Alice finished quickly, finding that she hadn't really left much out. Her dress, still dirty from last night, went on top and even with all of her school books for her holiday homework, she managed to close it easily. Under Adrianna's watchful eye, she didn't want to pack away her uniform, especially seeing that Adrianna's still hung in her closet. There was a chance that she was coming back next semester and she had to believe that it was a good one.

"When are your parents coming to get you?" Adrianna asked as they headed down for breakfast. Not many people seemed to even be awake yet, and those who made it out of their room were either completely calm or in a wild panic looking for things they needed to pack.

"Around one. You?"

Adrianna shook her head. "We're taking a plane tonight back home. Did you say one?"

"Yeah…"

Adrianna pointed out a clock as they entered the cafeteria. It was already noon.

They both grabbed something quick and portable before rushing back to their dorm room. Alice shoved the muffin in her mouth and chewed it along the way, swallowing and trying not to cough crumbs everywhere. Adrianna helped her go through the last bits of their room for anything else she might be missing.

"I think you got everything," Adrianna said, a small pile on her bed now of things they had found for her to pack away.

Alice tried to straighten out her hair, still a little wet from the shower, but left it down without a headband to hide the bruise on her temple. She looked over herself once more and decided that the tights, skirt and blouse were perfectly presentable for her father.

Adrianna handed her a jacket and pulled on her own, walking with Alice back to the spot where the parents were designated to pick up their children. Alice was glad she left her uniform behind, her suit case already plenty heavy enough without it. She couldn't even wheel it in the snow.

"Need a hand?" she heard from behind her. They both turned and Alice smiled up at Evan.

"Yes please," she said, handing her suitcase over to him.

He took it and carried it as he joined them. "Good first semester? Get a chance to go exploring? Stayed out of trouble?"

Alice nodded, careful not to push the hair out of her face. "Yes, thank you."

"That's good. I can think of a few people who didn't quite do that last one."

"They aren't that bad," Adrianna said. "It's not like they've gotten suspended or anything."

"I was thinking of Joe and Travis," Evan said. To Alice he added, "Ask them about the jello incident."

"Oh yeah," Adrianna said. "Does that mean Mike and Mark and Matt are ever going to stop?"

"One day. They can't be kids forever."

They reached the area where several students gathered, many of them currently being loaded into cars already. There were goodbyes happening already as couples gave one last kiss or friends exchanging hugs and well wishes for the holidays.

In the line-up of cars, she saw her mother sitting in the driver's seat of a red car she didn't recognize. Alice waved and her mother waved back, a bright smile spreading across her face as she opened the door and got out of the car.

Alice rushed towards her and waited on the curb.

"Did you have a good semester?" her mother asked, bending down to give Alice a hug.

Alice returned it. "It was great," she said, though her mind was elsewhere. "I had a lot of fun." She glanced back at Adrianna and Evan, both of them following after her, and asked her mother quietly, "Um… Am I going to…?"

"We didn't hear from the school once," her mother said, smiling brightly. "Your father is very happy about that."

"So I get to come back?"

Her mother nodded as Alice tried to contain herself.

"You should say goodbye to your friends," her mother said, nodding at Adrianna and Evan.

She turned and Adrianna swept her up in a hug. "Have a good Christmas!" she said.

"You too," Alice said, returning the hug and smiling.

Evan helped her mother put the suitcase into the trunk.

"Do you want me to bring your books back after the break?"

"Yes please," Alice said. Alice looked back at her mother and Evan before pulling Adrianna a little farther away and lowering her voice. "You can read them if you want if you promise not to tell anyone what's in them."

"I promise."

About the Author

TANYA LISLE IS a novelist from Metro Vancouver, British Columbia, who has series littered across genres from supernatural horror to young adult fantasy. She began writing in elementary school, when she started turning homework assignments into short stories and continued this trend well into university. While attending Simon Fraser University, she developed an appreciation for public domain crossovers and cross-platform narratives. She has a shelf full of note-books with more story ideas than pens lost to the depths of her bag. Now she writes incessantly in hopes of finishing all of them.

Thankfully, her cat, Remy, has figured out how to shut off Tanya's computer when she needs to take a break.